I think I was four the night she realized there might be something significant about my dream, the night I felt her body go stiff. I know I hadn't started school. I'd woken screaming as usual at some unearthly hour and she'd come and was holding me and I told her how I'd been standing at the top of some dark stairs and had fallen. She went stiff and pushed me out at arm's length, looking into my eyes.

'Who's been talking to you, Kirsty?' she asked. Her voice sounded funny and I was scared. 'Who was it darling?'

I didn't understand. I do now...

# ROBERT SWINDELLS

# Nightmare Stairs

CORGI

NIGHTMARE STAIRS

A CORGI BOOK 978 0 552 55590 6

First published in Great Britain by Doubleday, 1997
Reissued 2004, 2007

5 7 9 10 8 6 4

Copyright © Robert Swindells, 1997
Chapter head illustrations copyright © Angelo Rinaldi, 1997

The right of Robert Swindells to be identified as the author of this work has been
asserted in accordance with the Copyright, Designs and Patents Act 1988.

The Random House Group Limited supports the Forest Stewardship
Council (FSC®), the leading international forest certification organisation.
Our books carrying the FSC label are printed on FSC® certified paper. FSC
is the only forest certification scheme endorsed by the leading environmental
organisations, including Greenpeace. Our paper procurement policy can be
found at www.randomhouse.co.uk/environment

MIX
Paper from
responsible sources
FSC    FSC® C013604

Corgi Books are published by Random House Children's Books,
61–63 Uxbridge Road, London W5 5SA,
A Random House Group Company

Addresses for companies within The Random House Group Limited
can be found at: www.randomhouse.co.uk/offices.htm

THE RANDOM HOUSE GROUP Limited Reg. No. 954009
www.kidsatrandomhouse.co.uk

A CIP catalogue record for this book is available from the British Library.

Printed and bound by CPI Group (UK) Ltd, Croydon, CR0 4YY

*For Art and Catfish*

# CHAPTER ONE

Here's a riddle:

> *No vampire, ghost nor bug-a-boo*
> *I live and breathe and play, like you*
> *Yet I was murdered long ago*
> *Now tell me – how can this be so?*

Not easy, right? True though – every word.
If you're not doing anything special I'll tell you
all about it but I have to warn you – it's weird.
Seriously weird.

Listen.

# CHAPTER TWO

My first word was Mama. Well, whose isn't? It was my second word which caused a ripple, giving rise to one of those stories you find in every family. It goes like this.

I was fourteen months old, starting to toddle. Mum was dusting the room. She'd taken the framed photos off the sideboard and dumped them in an armchair. Family snaps. One was a black and white shot of Mum's parents in their garden. As Mum dusted the sideboard I was trying out my legs, lurching from one piece of furniture to another, and I arrived at this particular chair and picked up the photo. Mum saw me out of the corner of her eye and turned to take the thing away from me, afraid I might fall and smash the glass, and as she bent towards me I put my finger over my grandad's face and said, 'Bob.'

Not an earth-shattering event I admit, but it gave Mum a bit of a turn for two reasons. One, his name *had* been Bob, and two, both he and Grandma had died before I was born. I don't remember the incident myself, but apparently Mum gazed at me for a minute, dumb-founded, then shouted for Dad, and when Dad came I jabbed the same spot and said it again, quite distinctly. 'Bob.' Whereupon apparently they looked at me, then at each other, then burst out laughing. As I said, I remember nothing about it, but it seems they laughed so hard they had to hold each other up to keep from collapsing on the floor. They thought it was pure coincidence you see, because there was no way I could actually know the old guy's name. I was a baby, making baby noises, and twice I'd produced the same syllable which sounded remarkably like my late grandad's name.

And that's where they were wrong.

# CHAPTER THREE

I had nightmares. I'd wake up screaming and Mum would come. The nightmares were always about falling but she didn't know that. How could she when I hadn't learned to talk? You've heard the expression 'nameless fear', I suppose? Well, that's what *my* fear was back then. Nameless. Mum'd hold me. Rock me. Murmur words I didn't understand but was comforted by, till I went back to sleep.

As I grew older I learned the words for what frightened me at night. 'Falling,' I'd sob when I was two or three, clinging to my mother's nightie. 'Frightened. Hurts.' I understood what she was saying to me by then of course. 'Not falling,' she'd say. 'Mummy's got you. It was a dream, darling. Just a silly old dream.' God, she must have had the patience of a saint. Remember, this had been happening three, four times a week ever since I was born and she was always there. Always gentle.

I think I was four the night she realized there might be something significant about my dream, the night I felt her body go stiff. I know I hadn't started school. I'd woken screaming as usual at some unearthly hour and she'd come and was holding me and I told her how I'd been standing at the top of some dark stairs and had fallen.

She went stiff and pushed me out at arm's length, looking into my eyes. 'Who's been talking to you, Kirsty?' she asked. Her voice sounded funny and I was scared. 'Who was it, darling?'

I didn't understand. I do now, but I was *four*, for goodness' sake. I thought I'd done something terrible. She was hurting me too – holding my arms really tightly. I burst into tears. If I'd known then what I know now I'd have understood what was bugging her, but I didn't. When I started crying she hugged me and rocked me, and she never went stiff like that again in all the years that followed but all the same it was different somehow. Her

11

presence no longer consoled me quite as it had before. Presently I learned not to cry out on waking, and she and Dad thought my nightmare phase was at an end.

If only.

# CHAPTER FOUR

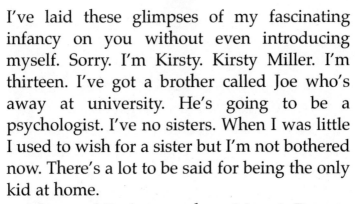

I've laid these glimpses of my fascinating infancy on you without even introducing myself. Sorry. I'm Kirsty. Kirsty Miller. I'm thirteen. I've got a brother called Joe who's away at university. He's going to be a psychologist. I've no sisters. When I was little I used to wish for a sister but I'm not bothered now. There's a lot to be said for being the only kid at home.

Mum and Dad are teachers. Mum is Deputy Head at Cutler's Hill Primary, where I was till a couple of years ago. *That*'s no fun, by the way – being a teacher's kid. The others think you're getting special treatment and they're right, but not the way they mean. I swear Mum picked on me all the time just to show I wasn't getting favours. Dad is Head of English at Bessamer

Comp which is *not* where I am, thank God. I'm at Fettler's.

I've mentioned my Grandad Bob, who's dead. He smoked sixty fags a day and that killed him. Forty-nine. Six foot tall. Four and a half stone. You can see it happening in the photo. That stoop. Those haunted eyes and sunken cheeks. A man who knows his days are numbered.

His wife – my mum's mum – was called Elizabeth. She lived twenty-one years as a widow and died ten months before I was born. She lived in Nine Beeches, the poshest part of Yaxley. You can see the front of the cottage behind her and Grandad in the snapshot. I've seen it in real life as well, but I'll save that story till later.

My other grandparents – Dad's mum and dad – are alive and kicking. Kath and Steve, they're called. My grandad's got an unusual job. He used to work in the steel industry, same as most people in Yaxley, but that's gone. Now he's at the airport, supervising a team that cleans out planes. I'm not kidding. It's a hectic job. They've ten minutes to remove every scrap of litter, hoover down the aisles, dispose of sick-bags, straighten magazines, take any unused meals from the galley and load it with fresh ones for the next flight. Ten minutes. The good thing about it is, he gets to keep the unused meals. You'd think they'd serve them on the next flight but they don't, so Steve and Kath practically live on airline food without ever leaving the ground.

And that's my family, except for my Auntie Anne. I haven't mentioned her yet because she's special. She deserves a page all to herself, and here it comes.

# CHAPTER FIVE

She's Mum's big sister, Auntie Anne, but they're not a bit alike. Or if they are *I* can't see it. Mum's nice, you know? A really nice person – the sort who'll go out of her way to do someone a good turn, even a complete stranger. Auntie Anne isn't. No way. I'll tell you the sort of person *she* is. Suppose she's in the car park and it's Saturday afternoon and the place is full, right? She's loaded her shopping into the boot and she's ready to leave when she notices someone waiting for her space. Instead of starting up and pulling away like she meant to, she'll find a cloth and get out and start working her way round the car, really slowly, doing the windows and mirrors. They don't *need* doing – she's making the guy wait, that's all. And if he gives up and moves on she's really glad. I know she's my auntie but I've no time for her. In fact I hate her and I always have.

Here's another family story. When I was about two days old, Mum gave me to Auntie Anne to hold. I'd been fed, burped and changed and was sleepily content, but the second my auntie took hold of me I started screaming and kicking. I made such a racket, Mum was scared I might blow myself to fragments. She snatched me out of her sister's arms and five seconds later I was fast asleep.

I bet Auntie Anne wasn't bothered. She's hardly the maternal type. She's married, but she and Uncle Brian have no kids. Anyway, that story is just another piece in the jigsaw I started putting together last summer. It builds into a pretty weird picture, as you'll find out.

# CHAPTER SIX

I was seven when we stopped to look at Grandma Elizabeth's old cottage. It was a Sunday in spring and we were out for a drive in the Volvo – Dad and Mum, Joe and me. I don't remember where we were going and it doesn't matter. Our route took us through Nine Beeches and Mum said something to Dad. He stopped the car and we got out.

'Oh look, Ken – they've *ruined* it,' groaned Mum as we peered over the gate at the house she'd grown up in. 'All those lovely old trees, gone. And look at that *hideous* dormer.' She pointed and I said, 'That's where the Glory Hole used to be.'

Mum glanced at me sharply. 'What?'

'The Glory Hole.' I could *see* it in my

mind's eye – a dim loft crammed with junk.

Mum squatted, her hands on my shoulders, gazing into my face. 'How do you know *that*, Kirsty? Who's talked to you about the cottage, darling?'

I shook my head. 'N-nobody's talked to me, Mum.'

'Oh, come on, Kirsty – somebody *must* have. How else would you know we called the loft the Glory Hole?'

Dad looked down at her. 'It could be any one of a number of people, Sylvia. Your sister. My parents. You might even have mentioned it yourself.'

She shook her head. 'I haven't, Ken. I *know* I haven't.'

'Well then, it must've been one of the others. It's not important, is it?'

'I – suppose not.' She straightened up and sighed. 'It's just . . . oh, I don't know. Can we leave, please? I wish we hadn't seen the place like this.'

We got back in the Volvo and drove on. Joe and I were fratching on the back seat and I suppose Mum thought I wouldn't hear when she murmured, 'There's something not quite right about that child, Ken.' She meant me of course, and I knew she was right. There *was* something not quite right about me, but five more years were to pass before I'd know what it was.

# CHAPTER SEVEN

Something not quite right. When I was eight we were doing World War Two at school. Mum wasn't my teacher that year. We had a man, Mr Newell. He was telling us about bombing. The Blitz, as it was called. When enemy bombers were coming a siren used to sound to warn people so they could get in their shelters. Mr Newell had a cassette with the siren on it. He put it on, and as soon as I heard that siren something happened to me. Something scary.

It was like a video switched on in my head. I was in this big dim place – a great high room full of people and – I don't know – machinery I guess. The siren was drawing a wavy line in the air. Everybody was moving towards these big doors. Lights were going out. The doors opened and everybody spilled out into a sort of yard. It was dark and cold and you could tell from the shiny paving that it had just stopped raining. I was watching all this but I was *there* too. I can't explain. Anyway we had to cross this yard and go down some stone stairs. Behind the siren was a droning noise and now and then a loud, flat bang. A finger of light was moving across the sky. I'd nearly reached the stairs when there was a terrific flash and something slammed into me so hard that I flew sideways into some bins or boxes or something. I cried out. At once the video shut off and I was back in the classroom with everybody staring.

Mr Newell had stopped the cassette player and was frowning across at me. 'Are you all right, Kirsty Miller?'

'Y-yes, sir.'

'Oh good. For a minute there I thought the bombs had got you.'

Everybody laughed.

At breaktime Sally came up to me. Sally Armitage, my best friend at Cutler's Hill. 'That was *great*,' she giggled. 'The siren, and this bloodcurdling scream at the end of it. I don't know how you *dared*.'

I shrugged and smiled. It hadn't been a case of daring, but I couldn't explain that to Sally. Not when I couldn't explain it to *myself*.

# CHAPTER EIGHT

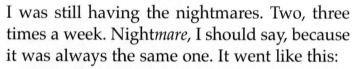

I was still having the nightmares. Two, three times a week. Night*mare*, I should say, because it was always the same one. It went like this:

I'm in the dark at the top of the stairs. Steep, narrow stairs. I have to get myself down those stairs but there's something wrong with my legs. They're stiff. It hurts me to walk. I'm standing there, sort of gathering myself to make the effort when I see movement out of the corner of my eye. Somebody or some*thing* comes out of the spare bedroom, fast and quiet. I don't even have time to feel scared. Whoever or whatever it is puts a hand or paw in the middle of my back and shoves and I topple forward, crashing down the stairs in a chaos of terror, shock and pain.

I never hit the bottom. I wake up, damp and

shaking. For a short time I can actually feel the pain, hear the crashing row my falling body makes. I lie gasping, knowing that if I ever reach the foot of the stairs asleep, I'll never wake.

Sometimes in the evenings I'd overhear Mum and Dad talking. What kid doesn't? Mostly it was stuff I wasn't interested in. Money. Relatives. People at work. Stuff that happened years ago before I was born. Now and then though, I'd overhear something that'd ring a bell. A distant bell.

Like the night Mum got on to the war. We'd just watched an old film about London in the Blitz. I'd gone through to the kitchen to put the kettle on and I heard Mum say to Dad, 'They show the explosions and the fires and the falling buildings, but you never see what it *did* to people – how their lives were ruined. Take my mother – hit by the blast the night they bombed Viner's. Knocked her halfway across the yard. Smashed her legs. Fifteen, she was. Fifteen, and she never walked again without pain.'

Yeah, you've got it. My one-girl video show

two years back in old Newell's class. I'd forgotten all about it, but it came back with a bang that night, I can tell you. My heart kicked me in the ribs. I swallowed. Went cold. I made the tea and when I carried it through Mum'd switched channels, but I didn't enjoy the stuff we gawped at after that. Couldn't concentrate.

# CHAPTER NINE

Now and then Mum and Dad have to attend the same meeting after school. I hate it because I have to have my tea at Auntie Anne's and wait there till they come for me. She doesn't like me, my Auntie Anne. Oh, she pretends, but I can tell. Anyway, it just so happened that there was one of these meetings two days after I overheard the bit about Grandma Elizabeth and the bomb, and I made the mistake of mentioning it.

Well, it had been preying on my mind. Was it just coincidence, that strange experience I'd had when I was eight, or was it possible I'd seen a bit out of Grandma Elizabeth's life? I'd spent two nights lying awake thinking about it. In fact it was doing my head in. I felt I had to share it with somebody or go crazy. So when tea was over and Uncle Brian left the table and went upstairs I took a deep breath and plunged in.

'Auntie Anne?'

'Yes?' She looked at me over the rim of her cup. She had these very thin, plucked eyebrows and lots of green and purple eyeliner. Made her look like Queen Whatsit. Nefertiti.

'D'you think ... is it possible for someone to see into the past?'

She shook her head. 'No, Kirsty, it is not. The past is over and done with. Why d'you ask?'

'Oh, I ... something happened at school once. Ages ago. I thought I saw a bit of Grandma's life.' I shrugged. 'Can't have, can I?'

'Grandma's life?' She lowered her cup into its saucer without taking her eyes off my face. 'Your Grandma Kath?'

I shook my head. 'Grandma Elizabeth.'

She sniffed. 'You never *knew* Grandma Elizabeth, Kirsty. How could you possibly see any part of *her* life?'

I pulled a face. 'I dunno. It's daft. We were doing about the war. The teacher had this tape.' I told her what had happened when the siren went. She listened, her bottom lip caught between her teeth. I noticed that some of her lipstick had got onto her two front teeth. When I'd finished she said, 'Imagination, Kirsty, that's all it was. The lesson caught your imagination and you felt as if you were *there*, just for a minute.'

I nodded. 'Yes, but then a couple of nights ago we watched this film about the war, and Mum mentioned something that happened to Grandma Elizabeth and it was the *same*. Exactly the same. My legs. *Her* legs, I mean.'

She got up then, so suddenly it made me jump. Her face looked white, though that might have been my imagination too. 'Nonsense,' she rapped. 'Nobody sees the past. It's gone, dear. Dead and gone.'

She didn't mean the *dear* bit, I can tell you. She turned her back and started crashing dishes in the sink and it was obvious I'd upset her. After a minute I got up and grabbed a tea towel and she said, 'Leave them to drain, please.' Snapped at me, you know? So I rehung the flipping tea towel and stalked off into her immaculate front room to watch the telly. Neither of us mentioned the matter when Mum and Dad came for me but they *must've* felt the atmosphere. So. Telling someone hadn't helped a bit, and I hated going to my auntie's even more after that.

# CHAPTER TEN

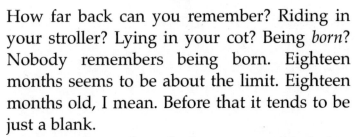

How far back can you remember? Riding in your stroller? Lying in your cot? Being *born*? Nobody remembers being born. Eighteen months seems to be about the limit. Eighteen months old, I mean. Before that it tends to be just a blank.

Not with me though. I can remember being – what – a few minutes old? An hour or two? I *think* I can anyway.

You know the nightmare I told you about? Standing at the top of the stairs and being shoved and falling? And I said I always wake up before I hit the bottom? Well, that's not quite true. Not quite. Sometimes – just now and then – I stay asleep a bit longer and the dream goes on, and that's where it gets really scary. I don't even want to talk about it but I've got to because that's where the last piece is. The last piece of the jigsaw, I mean.

What happens is this. I'm falling. Everything's whirling, crashing, pain. Then suddenly it's still and quiet and there's this – fading away. Everything's fading away. The fear. The light. The pain. I'm sinking into warm soft darkness where things don't matter any more and it's really, really restful and I want it to go on for ever and ever, and just when I think it's going to there's noise again, and pain, and flashes of light that hurt my eyes and all of this goes on for oh, I don't know how long. It stops eventually, and then I'm lying on my back and there's this great fuzzy brightness and it's really cold and there's something rough against my skin and everything – hurts. There's movement – things moving, but I can't see properly. Everything's fuzzy. I think, *Is this Heaven? Hell?* I'm scared. I don't seem to be able to move much. Can't get up. I reach out my hand and it finds something. A warm thing, but hard. I curl my fingers round it. Hold on to it. Something moves in front of the light. It swoops, becoming a face. A face I don't know, smiling into mine and that's when I realize I'm a baby. *That* wakes me up, I can tell you.

And then they wonder why newborn babies howl.

# CHAPTER ELEVEN

It must've hit you by now what's happened. What I'm saying. I'm saying Kirsty Miller's been here before. Have you never heard anybody say that about a new baby? Sometimes a baby'll get this look in its eyes – a deep, *knowing* look – and somebody'll say, 'Oooh, look at that – *she's* been here before.' Well, what I'm saying is, they're probably right without knowing it.

Oh yes, I know it's far-fetched. I realize that. It was months before *I* could get my head round it but, you see, the evidence was all there. I knew the layout of the cottage at Nine Beeches, though I'd never been inside. I knew its loft used to be known as the Glory Hole. I knew Grandad Rodwell's first name – Bob – though nobody had ever used the name in my hearing. And I knew exactly what had happened to Grandma Elizabeth the night they bombed Viner's – I'd seen it, *felt* it, without ever leaving my seat in Mr Newell's class at Cutler's Hill Primary. And I was pretty sure I knew something else as well – something terrible, which nobody knew but me and a certain other person.

I struggled with all this stuff for months. Wrestled it in bed at night. I was desperate to tell someone but I didn't dare. Especially not the last bit – the awful suspicion I harboured about a member of my family. I was afraid that if I told anyone they'd think I was crazy and have me committed to one of those psychiatric hospitals they never let you out of. And I actually *felt* crazy. I wasn't sleeping. Couldn't concentrate at school. It felt like my life was crumbling. Falling apart. I had to *do* something.

One Saturday last autumn – it was the start of the October break – I was helping Mum with the vegetables. Dad was outside doing something to the car. I was at breaking point – really tensed up, and I said, 'Mum – how did Grandma Elizabeth die?' They'd never talked

35

about it, see? Not in my hearing. All I knew was that she'd died a few months before I was born.

Mum gave me a funny look. 'What made you think about *that* all of a sudden, darling?' All of a sudden. That's a laugh for a start. I pulled a face. 'I think I know anyway, Mum. She fell downstairs, didn't she?'

'Who told you that, Kirsty?'

'Nobody. It happened at the cottage, didn't it? At Nine Beeches?'

'*Somebody* must have told you, or you wouldn't know. *I* certainly never mentioned it. Was it Auntie Anne?'

I shook my head. 'I *told* you, Mum – it was nobody. I just – know, that's all. Why is it such a secret anyway? A lot of old people die falling downstairs.'

Mum nodded. 'I know, darling, but you see – there was your nightmare. Do you remember your nightmare? About falling? You used to get it almost every night. Your dad and I thought if you knew your grandma died from a fall it might make your nightmare worse. Sounds silly now but we did, and that's why we never mentioned it.'

I shook my head. 'I doubt if it'd have made

any difference to my nightmare, Mum. Anyway you can tell me now, 'cause I know already.'

She shrugged. 'There's really nothing to tell, darling. Your grandma's legs were bad because of the war. She shouldn't have stayed on at the cottage after your grandad died but she wouldn't give it up. The staircase was steep and dark. One day she must have slipped or tripped or something, at the top. The postman found her next morning. He had a package for her, and when she didn't answer his knock he looked through the slot and there she was at the foot of the stairs. Her neck was broken. The doctor said she would have died instantly.'

She didn't, I thought. Not quite. There was no pain, but she felt everything going away.

'Poor Grandma,' I murmured, scraping diced carrots into the pan with the back of the knife. 'Dying alone like that.'

Alone my foot, I thought, lighting the gas. It was amazing how angry I felt.

# CHAPTER TWELVE

Who was my anger directed at? Go on – have a guess. If you think it was directed at Auntie Anne, you're absolutely right. Well done.

I've told you a bit about my auntie. She's the one who'll hang on to a parking space for the pleasure of screwing up a total stranger. She's also the one in my dream who comes out of the spare bedroom and shoves me off the top step.

Oh yes. Of course I didn't realize till last summer. Or maybe I'd known all along but wouldn't let myself believe it. Because it is sort of unbelievable, isn't it? Her own *mother*, for goodness' sake.

In case you think I was jumping to conclusions – branding Auntie Anne a murderer on the strength of a dream and a coincidence –

I'd better tell you something I forgot before. Remember I said we stopped once when I was seven to look at Grandma's old cottage? And Joe and I were fratching on the back seat while Mum and Dad chuntered on, and I heard Mum say, *There's something not quite right about that child*. Remember? Right. Well, Dad said something too. About the cottage. I didn't get it at the time, but I do now. By golly I do. This is what he said: *It's a pity your mother didn't get around to changing her will. If she had, we'd be living in the cottage and that ugly dormer would never have been built.*

Well. Doesn't take a university education, does it? To sort that one out, I mean. Those words of Dad's came back to me when Mum said Grandma ought not to have stayed on at the cottage. I didn't say anything. Not straight away. I went up to my room and had a think, and then I asked Mum another question, and her answer completed the jigsaw.

'Mum?' We'd eaten the meal. Mum and I were doing the dishes. Dad was in the front room, watching sport.

'Yes, dear?'

'What did Dad mean when he said it's a

pity Grandma Elizabeth didn't change her will?'

She frowned. 'When did he say that, Kirsty? *I* don't remember.'

'Oh, it was years ago. In the car. What did he mean?'

Mum sighed. 'Well, I really don't understand why you're interested, dear, but if you must know it was like this. Your grandma's will left the cottage to Auntie Anne as the elder daughter, but when Grandma learned that Anne and Brian didn't intend having children, she decided to change her will so that I would get it. We had Joe, you see, and were trying for a girl. Unfortunately she didn't get around to it straightaway, and then she had her accident and that was that.'

Makes you think, doesn't it? Made *me* think.

# CHAPTER THIRTEEN

As I've said, it was October break. I'd just
finished my first half-term at Fettler's, which
hadn't been easy with all this stuff building up
inside my head. Anyway, it meant I had a
week, and I decided to spend it looking for
evidence of Auntie Anne's guilt.

I'd no idea how to begin. I wondered what
would happen if I simply confronted her. *I
know your secret, Auntie Anne. You murdered
your mother to get the cottage, didn't you?* Would
she break down? Confess? Great if she did, but
what if she didn't? What if she got blazingly
angry, ordered me out of her house and called
Dad? *Kirsty's flipped her lid.* And what if I'm
wrong after all and she's completely innocent?

No, I couldn't proceed that way. I couldn't

confide in anybody either. I spent most of Sunday sitting on a bench in Yaxley town centre, thinking. Everything was shut so I had the place practically to myself. At three o'clock it started to drizzle and I moved into C&A's doorway. There was this dummy in the window – a guy in a dark suit with a briefcase, reading the *Financial Times*, and that's what gave me the idea. It'd be in the paper, wouldn't it, when my grandma was found dead? Not the *Financial Times* of course, but the *Yaxley Star*. It was full of stuff like that. I could go to the public library and look through back numbers of the paper. I knew roughly when it happened. Ten months before I was born. I was born in April 1984, so Grandma Elizabeth must've died sometime in June 1983. So, all I had to do was look through every edition of the *Star* for that month and I'd find it. Of course it might not tell me anything I didn't already know but on the other hand it might, and anyway I had to start somewhere.

I couldn't do it that day because the library doesn't open Sundays. I walked home through the rain feeling better than I had for months.

Not terrific, you know, but better. At least now I was *doing* something instead of just brooding, but if I'd known what I was letting myself in for, I think I might have left it alone.

# CHAPTER FOURTEEN

A funny thought came into my head in bed that night. Funny peculiar, not funny ha-ha. Here it is. Grandma Elizabeth was Mum's mother, so if I was her reincarnation *I* was Mum's mother too, in a way. I was hers and she was mine. Wonder what she'd say if I told her?

Needless to say, I didn't. Next morning I walked into town and went to the library. I'd pictured myself sitting with a stack of fusty old papers, turning hundreds and hundreds of yellow-edged pages and sneezing from the dust, but it wasn't like that at all. Instead I found myself sitting in front of a contraption with a screen, a bit like a computer monitor. All the papers have been photographed in miniature on like film. All you have to do is feed the film through the machine and pages come up on screen. Microfiche, it's called. You operate it by hand so you can go as fast or as slow as you want. Once you know how to do it it's dead easy, and far better than searching through actual papers.

So there I sat, feeding and reading. I got distracted a few times, like there was this piece about a spacecraft, *Pioneer 10*, which had become the first man-made object to travel beyond the solar system. I stopped and read it because I'm into stuff like that, but I found what I was looking for too.

June 14th 1983. That's when the postman found her, so she probably died on the 13th, which struck me as appropriate. It was a short piece – ten or twelve lines. I'd brought a notebook and I copied the item into it, word for word. I could probably have asked for a photocopy or something, but I didn't want people knowing what I was doing. Here's what it said:

## WIDOW FOUND DEAD

*An elderly woman was found dead at her home in Nine Beeches today after apparently falling downstairs. Mrs Elizabeth Rodwell, a widow, lived alone. Her body was discovered by postman Mr Derek Lassiter, who peered through the letter slot after Mrs Rodwell failed to answer his knock. Mr Lassiter contacted the police but a spokesman told our reporter, 'There'll be an inquest, but as far as we are concerned this was a domestic tragedy. There is no question of foul play.'*

*Mrs Rodwell was the mother of Mrs Anne Tasker, well known locally as manager of Whiteleys estate agency. She also leaves a second daughter, and one grandchild.*

That was it. The only surprise was that bit about Auntie Anne and Whiteleys. The place is still there but my aunt has no connection with it, and it was news to me she ever did. I underlined it in my notebook and scrolled through nine more copies of the *Star* till I located a report of the inquest. Death by misadventure, the coroner had decided. I jotted it down, wondering if this was the only time the guy'd been wrong. Then I left the library. I felt like Sherlock flipping Holmes, except he'd probably have known what to do next and I didn't.

# CHAPTER FIFTEEN

I went to Island in the shopping mall. It's a coffee bar. I got a Coke and sat at a corner table, thinking.

What am I trying to do? Easy – prove that my Auntie Anne pushed her mother downstairs. All right – what proof do I have so far? Answer – none at all. There's my dream of course, but I doubt whether that would impress the police. Can't you just see it?

*Sergeant, you've got to arrest my auntie.*

*Oh, and why's that, Miss?*

*She murdered my grandma.*

*Did she now? How d'you know?*

*I dreamed it. And anyway I was my grandma. In a previous life.*

Non-starter, right? So. I need *proof.* Something solid. What I really need to find out is what Auntie Anne was doing on June 13th 1983 – the day Grandma fell downstairs. Trouble is, it was fourteen years ago. Who's going to remember? *She* will, but I can hardly ask her, can I? Uncle Brian might, but I can't ask him either.

All right – what do I know already? Well, I know it was a Monday because the story was in Tuesday's *Star*. So it was a working day. And I know Anne was managing Whiteleys, so presumably she was there. Was anybody there *with* her? And if someone was, is that person still working at Whiteleys now? Doubt it. Fourteen years ago. But it's a start, isn't it? Something to do. Go along to Whiteleys and ask. Make enquiries, like a private detective.

They were having a slow day at Whiteleys. No customers. There was just this guy behind the counter. Plumpish, thirty-something, ginger moustache, and a woman in a glass cubicle behind with a VDU. 'Yes?' goes the guy as I walk through the door. No enthusiasm – I'm too young to be looking for a house.

'I – wonder if you can help me?'

He smiles faintly. 'Depends. School project, is it?'

'No. I'm looking for someone.'

'We do homes, petal, not missing persons.' Ignorant pig.

'It's someone who might have worked here with my auntie, fourteen years ago.'

'Fourteen *years*?' He shakes his head. 'Fourteen years ago I was living in Exeter, darling. How would *I* know about somebody who worked here then?'

I glance past his shoulder. 'Perhaps that lady . . . ?'

'No chance. She's been here three weeks.'

'Oh. Well . . . do you keep records – you know . . . ?'

'No records, sweetheart. Just houses. Look.' He spreads his pudgy palms on the counter and leans towards me. 'You're wasting your time, which probably doesn't matter, and mine, which does. Why don't you go away and come back when you're looking for somewhere to live, *then* we might be able to help you.'

I'm the quiet type, you know? Hate making any kind of fuss, but this guy is so obnoxious –

so *slimy* – that I gaze into his piggy little eyes and say, 'You must be joking. I'd live in a rubbish skip before I'd come to a plonker like you.' I flounce out before his tiny brain can think up a reply.

# CHAPTER SIXTEEN

Mum might know if anybody worked with Anne. They're sisters after all, but how can I ask her? She doesn't even know I know about my auntie's job at Whiteleys. If she finds out I'm prying into Anne's life she's going to want to know why, and I couldn't possibly explain.

What about Anne herself? Might it be possible to raise the subject of her past life casually, in the course of conversation? It wouldn't be easy. Auntie Anne and I don't *have* conversations. I don't even go near her house except when Mum and Dad have meetings, but I couldn't think of any other way, so I decided to give it a go.

What I did was, I pretended to be worried about my future. In actual fact I didn't give a hoot about my future, but Auntie Anne wasn't to know that. I sat in her neat shiny lounge and gave her some bull about the careers teacher at school asking us all what we wanted to be and me being the only girl who didn't know. I said I'd tried talking to Mum about it, but she'd said it was too soon to start worrying – I was only thirteen, for goodness' sake. Anne said, 'Your mother's right, Kirsty. It is too soon. You should be enjoying yourself while you can.'

I nodded. 'I know, but . . .' I looked at her. 'Have *you* ever had a job, Auntie Anne?' Dead innocent.

She nodded. 'Oh yes. More than one.'

'What were they?'

'Well – when I was sixteen I worked at a hairdresser's as a trainee. It didn't suit me so I moved to a fashion shop. I started as junior sales and rose to manageress at nineteen. I stayed there till I was twenty-two, then Whiteleys the estate agents opened their branch in Yaxley and advertised for a manager.' She smiled. 'They wanted a man really but I applied and was interviewed, and they must have been impressed because I got the job.' She smirked. 'Good salary, commission, company car. Not bad for a woman of twenty-two.' She's dead modest, my auntie. I hate her. I felt like saying, *Hmmm – a manager at twenty-two, then a murderer. Quite a career.* That'd have shut her up.

'Wow!' I pulled a face. 'I bet it was hard though. Did you have people under you? You know – staff?'

She smiled wryly. 'Staff'd be a bit of an exaggeration, Kirsty. I had Molly. Oh, and a woman who cleaned the place three evenings a week.'

'What did Molly do?'

My auntie shrugged. 'Secretarial work. Typing. Filing. Keeping the appointments book, answering the phone.'

'Is that a good job?'

Anne shook her head. 'No, not really. You want to set your sights a bit higher than Molly Barraclough, Kirsty.'

'Yes but *what*, Auntie Anne? Every job the teacher mentions sounds really boring. I want to do something interesting or exciting. D'you think travel agency work . . . ?'

It went on like that for a while, but I'd got

what I came for. The hardest bit was remembering the name while Auntie Anne went banging on. The minute I got outside I wrote it in my notebook.

Molly Barraclough.

# CHAPTER SEVENTEEN

Tuesday morning. Dad had dashed off to some meeting. Mum and I were dossing over the breakfast table in our dressing gowns, sipping coffee. Mum was reading a letter from someone she was at college with.

'Mum?'

'Uh-huh?' She didn't look up.

'Who's Molly Barraclough?'

'Huh? I'm sorry, darling, *who* did you say?'

'Molly Barraclough.'

Now she glanced up. 'Where on earth did you hear Molly's name, Kirsty? I haven't seen Molly for ... oh, must be ten years. Longer, probably.'

'Auntie Anne mentioned her once,' I lied truthfully.

'Hmm,' grunted Mum. 'Did she blush?'

'How d'you mean?'

Mum folded her letter and put it down. 'Molly worked for your auntie when she was manager at Whiteleys. Did you know Auntie Anne used to be a manager, darling?'

'Uh . . . I think she told me.'

'I bet she didn't tell you that when poor Molly started with multiple sclerosis she sacked her out of hand.' Mum pulled a face. 'Makes you a bit clumsy, MS. You drop things, knock things over.'

'So Auntie Anne sacked her?'

Mum nodded. 'Yes. She was a sweetie too. Always cheerful. I used to run into her sometimes in town after she left Whiteleys. She was living on the Flower Estate then but perhaps she moved away, or died.' She sighed. 'That's how it is, Kirsty – we come and we go. More coffee?'

Slow stuff, detective work. I helped with the dishes, then went to my room and wrote 'Flower Estate' in my notebook, next to Molly's name. It's called the Flower Estate because all the roads are named after wild flowers. It's a big sprawling place on a hillside. I was praying Mum was wrong – that

Molly Barraclough hadn't gone away.

I waited till I heard Mum start hoovering the front room, then slipped downstairs and got the phone book. I sat on my bed and looked up Barraclough. Turned out there were hundreds of Barracloughs in Yaxley – nearly two pages. I went straight to the initial M. There were seventeen M. Barracloughs, but I struck lucky because only three of them lived in Cattercliff, the district that includes the Flower Estate, and one of *them* wasn't on the estate itself.

So, two possibilities. I copied the numbers and addresses into my notebook. M. Barraclough of 22 Celandine Nook, and M. Barraclough of 34 Ragwort Drive. No way of knowing which was Molly. Neither, probably. Anyway, I'd call and ask for Molly. What I'd do if I got her I'd no idea.

# CHAPTER EIGHTEEN

I didn't phone from home. Too risky. I went down town, to the library. They've got a row of public phones.

I called Celandine Nook. A woman picked up. 'Oh hello,' I said. 'Is this Molly Barraclough?'

'You must have the wrong number. There's no Molly here.' She hung up before I could apologize.

A woman answered at Ragwort Drive too. 'Oh hello,' I chirped. 'Am I speaking to Molly Barraclough?'

'Ye-es. Who is this?'

My heart kicked. I swallowed. 'Were you . . . did you once work at Whiteleys on Steeler Street?'

'That's right. Who's speaking please?'

'You don't know me, Ms Barraclough, but Anne Tasker is my auntie.'

'Anne . . . ? Oh, yes. Anne. So how can I help you, love?'

'I wondered if I could have a word with you.'

'What about?'

'About my auntie. Something that happened.'

'I'm sorry, I don't understand. Something that happened?'

'Well . . . something that *might* have happened, fourteen years ago. Something serious.'

'I still don't understand, dear. What's your name, by the way?'

'Oh, sorry. It's Kirsty. Kirsty Miller.'

'How old are you, Kirsty?'

'Thirteen. Look – it's *really* important, honestly. Couldn't we meet somewhere? In town?

'I – don't get out much these days. Trouble walking.'

'Oh, I'm sorry. Would it be OK if I came to see you? I know where you are.'

'Well . . . I suppose so, but I have to say

I'm mystified. When were you thinking of coming?'

'Oh, whenever's best for you, Ms Barraclough. No school this week.'

'Well – how would two o'clock this afternoon suit you?'

'That'd be fantastic.'

She chuckled. 'I can't promise it'll be fantastic, love, but there *is* a packet of chocolate biscuits somewhere if I can find it. Two o'clock, then?'

'On the dot. And thanks a lot.'

'A poet too, eh?' She chuckled again and hung up. I looked at my watch. Ten past ten. What could I usefully do for three hours or so? Sherlock Holmes would've done some opium and played his violin. I settled for coffee and piped music at Island.

# CHAPTER NINETEEN

I bussed it out to the Flower Estate and found Ragwort Drive. Number 34 could have done with a paint job and the garden sorting. I took a deep breath, marched up the weedy path and knocked.

It took her ages to answer. When the door finally opened I found myself looking at a plumpish woman of about forty in a purple sweater and black leggings. She had a mop of frizzy grey hair and was propped on a single elbow-crutch. She smiled. 'Kirsty?'

'Y-yes. I'm sorry to . . .'

'It's all right, love. Come on in.' She swivelled a half turn on the crutch, making room. 'Through there. Sit yourself down. I'll be with you in a minute.' She shut the door and moved off along the hallway. I entered the living room, where a pair of two-seater settees took up most of the space. There was a low table with a TV and video, a gas fire, a glass and steel coffee table with a stack of news-papers and magazines at one end, a small bookcase, and in a corner a weeping fig in a square white tub. The blue carpet was faded and threadbare, especially round the doorway. I sat down on one of the settees and looked at a print of Salisbury Cathedral on the wall.

She came in, balancing a loaded tray in one trembling hand. I jumped up and took it, going, 'You should've . . . I would've . . .'

''S OK, love, thanks. Put it on the coffee table. That's right. Now.' She lowered herself into the other settee, laid the crutch along the floor and smiled. 'We'll have a nice cuppa, and you can tell me what this is about.'

Back at Island, I'd thought about how I might handle this. I'd decided it'd be best not to mention dreams and trances and stuff if I could help it, and certainly not reincarnation. I didn't want this woman thinking she'd let some sort of nutcase into her home. I wondered if I should offer to pour the tea, but disabled people can be sensitive about – you know – people thinking they can't do stuff, so in the end I left her to it. We sat, sipping tea and nibbling chocolate biscuits, and I said, 'I'm interested in the thirteenth and fourteenth of June 1983.'

Molly gave me a look. Half-smiling, half-quizzical. 'Are you now? As precise as that. Why?'

'Because that's when my grandma died.'

'Your grandma?'

I nodded. 'Elizabeth Rodwell, Ms Barra-clough. Anne's mother.'

'Ah. Ah, yes.' She became still. Her eyes had a distant look and I knew she was somewhere else. In her cubicle at Whiteleys, perhaps. I waited, gazing at her. After a minute she came back, murmuring, 'I remember. Of course I do. How strange, after all this time.' She looked at me. 'She fell downstairs, didn't she? Your grandma, I mean.'

I nodded. My heart was racing. I hoped she couldn't tell. 'That's what I was told. It was before I was born, you see. Ten months before.'

'Yes.' She was holding her cup with the fingertips of both hands, gazing into it like someone reading the leaves. 'Why have you come to me? Why me? Surely your family . . . your mother . . .' She looked straight at me. 'What exactly are you looking for, Kirsty?'

I swallowed. What could I say? I shrugged. 'I . . . I'm not sure, Ms Barraclough. I . . .'

'Molly,' she corrected. 'Call me Molly.' She fixed me with her level gaze. 'You think . . . you suspect there was something unusual about your grandmother's death, don't you?' Her voice was soft, almost a whisper. I didn't say anything. I couldn't. All my life I'd been the only one. The sole custodian of a truly dreadful suspicion. Or that's what I'd always assumed. Now it seemed I might have been mistaken. Now there was Molly and suddenly it was out in the open, lying like some repulsive object in the silence between us. I tore my eyes from hers and stared at the carpet, my lower lip caught between my teeth. I could feel her looking at me. Looking at me.

I nodded.

# CHAPTER TWENTY

'Ah.' She sipped some tea, watching me over the rim of the cup. I gazed into mine, thinking, if I don't say anything else – if I get up now and leave – it needn't go any further. It'll be a suspicion shared by two people, that's all. There'll be no need to *do* anything. But if I speak, my words will make it real, and then . . .

'What do you think happened, Kirsty?' She spoke softly. I felt her eyes on me. I looked at her.

'I think . . . I believe my aunt pushed my grandma, Molly.' There. It was out. Events would follow now. Consequences. It was inevitable.

Molly nodded. 'I believe so too, Kirsty. Always have. It was all too – convenient, you see. The way it worked out, I mean.'

'Convenient?'

She nodded. 'Yes. I think that's the right word.' She leaned forward, put her cup and saucer on the table and settled back, her right arm along the padded arm of the chair, her left in her lap. 'I might as well start at the beginning and tell you exactly what happened on those two days in 1983.' She sighed. 'I can't tell you how hard I've tried to forget about all of this over the years, Kirsty. It's haunted me, and perhaps this is why. Perhaps you were always meant to seek me out, with your big blue eyes and your disturbing questions.' She shrugged. 'Well anyway, this is how it was.

'One day in early June of 1983, a man came into the office. His name was Mr Abubaka Tefawa Shah.' Molly smiled. 'That name – Abubaka Tefawa Shah – is one of the reasons I've not been able to forget the incident in spite of my best endeavours. It's memorable. Sticks in the mind. And it wasn't just the name. He was a striking figure, Kirsty. Not the sort of man you normally come across in Yaxley. You could tell he was rich by the way he carried himself. His haircut. The way he spoke. And his clothes. The best, Kirsty. The very best.

Clothes like his place their wearer, just as this crummy sweater places me. Anyway, Mr Shah was anxious to acquire a property in Nine Beeches. It *must* be Nine Beeches – he wasn't interested in any other location.' She smiled. 'And as luck would have it, we hadn't anything in Nine Beeches at the time. Not a thing.

'Your aunt was distraught. Well – she could see as well as I could that Mr Shah would pay any price for what he wanted. It was a case of money no object, and your aunt was more than usually fond of money, Kirsty, if you'll forgive my saying so. She was desperate not to let this walking gold mine walk away, so she told him we were expecting something to come vacant any day. Leave your card, she said, and we'll call you as soon as things start moving. So he gave her a card and went off. I was sure we'd seen the last of him, because we weren't expecting anything in Nine Beeches at all. She'd lied to him about that, or I thought she had, but then—' Molly broke off, groping for the elbow-crutch. 'Look – I'm parched. Why don't I brew a fresh pot? You must be fed up of listening to me anyway.'

'No no, I'm not, but if you're parched, *I'll* make tea—'

'No you won't.' She hauled herself erect and leaned on the stick. 'You can bring the tray though, if you want to help.'

I didn't want to help. I didn't want tea. I wanted to hear the rest of the story, though I imagined I could guess most of it. Anyway, Molly was stumping towards the door so I picked up the tray and followed her.

# CHAPTER TWENTY-ONE

When we'd settled ourselves with steaming cups and the last of the biscuits, Molly said, 'Now – where was I?'

'Mr Shah,' I prompted. 'He'd left his card.'

'Ah, yes. Well, a few days went by – about a week, I suppose – and then one afternoon your aunt stuck her head round my door and said she was popping out for a while. It wasn't unusual – she often did bits of shopping in office hours or had her hair done, so I didn't think anything of it. But when she came back a couple of hours later she told me to call Mr Shah and ask him to pop into the office when he'd got a minute, because she'd found a property at Nine Beeches he might be interested in. Now, there wasn't anything particularly strange about that, except there was nothing in the appointments book.' Molly broke off, sipped some tea and explained. 'You see, what normally happened was, somebody wanting to sell their house would phone Whiteleys and arrange for your aunt to go and view the property, explain our terms and so forth, and I'd write the appointment in the book. Well, I couldn't remember writing anything about Nine Beeches, and I *would* have remembered because of Mr Shah. So later, after I'd called him, I checked, and there was nothing. I was a bit puzzled, but I told myself Anne must have taken a call while I was at lunch or something and fixed the appointment herself, without writing it down. That would have been unusual but it had happened from time to time so I put it out of my mind, until next morning when she rang me at nine to say she'd be late, her mother had been found dead.'

Molly stopped and I murmured, 'Her mother was found on the fourteenth, but Anne knew about the cottage on the thirteenth – is *that* what you're saying?'

Molly nodded. I stared at the carpet for a few seconds, then looked at her. 'Why . . . why didn't you say something at the time, Molly? Mention it to somebody – the police? Surely there'd have been clues. Evidence.'

She shook her head. 'The postman called the police. It was they who broke in, found that your grandma was dead. If there'd been anything suspicious they'd have spotted it, but no.' She smiled tightly. 'Your aunt committed the perfect murder, Kirsty. That's what I've always believed, anyway.'

I nodded. Neither of us spoke for a while. I don't know what Molly was thinking, but I was wondering what I ought to do next. I mean, there'd be no proof now, would there? Not after fourteen years, but you can't just *leave* something like that, can you? You can't carry on with your life, knowing murder was committed. Having tea at the murderer's house, chatting with her about this and that. Especially when you were the victim in a previous life.

Molly broke the silence, clearing her throat. 'And you, Kirsty. What was it made you suspect your aunt?'

Ah well, I thought. It had to come. The six million dollar question. Now she finds out I'm bonkers. I pulled a face. 'I have this dream. This nightmare. Somebody shoves me downstairs. I've had it since I was a baby.'

Molly smiled, a Mona Lisa smile. I'd expected her to flip. Yell at me. Chuck me out of her house, but instead she smiled, like smiling at a secret thought, and she nodded. 'You're a dreamer too,' she murmured. 'I thought so.' Her smile broadened. 'Takes one to know one, as they say.'

I stared at her. 'You mean, you . . . ?'

'Oh, yes. I dream. Always have.' She spread her arms and looked down at herself. 'I even knew I was going to wind up like this, only I blocked it out. Didn't want to know. So you see, I know exactly how you feel.'

I didn't know what to say, my head was in such a whirl. 'That's great,' I stammered. 'I mean, not that you're . . . you know, but to know I'm not the only one. I thought I was going crazy—' I broke off, then ploughed on. Might as well get it over. Drag it into the open, see what happens. I pulled a face. 'Trouble is, there's more, Molly. Not just the dreaming, and if I tell you everything you *will* think I'm loopy. I know you will.'

Molly shook her head. 'I doubt it, Kirsty. Try me.'

So I did.

# CHAPTER TWENTY-TWO

She didn't say anything for a while when I'd finished. I don't blame her. I mean, reincarnation. Takes some swallowing, right? She seemed to be concentrating on her tea, but I knew the old brainbox must be working overtime. I left her to it and stared at the rug, sipping now and then from my cup. I was doing my Sherlock Holmes bit again, weighing alternatives. It went something like this:

You can't choose to do nothing. Not now. So, you've got to prove that Auntie Anne murdered her mother.

There are two ways of bringing a criminal to justice. You either produce strong evidence – fingerprints, fibres – something that places the suspect at the scene of the crime – or you get a confession. You're not going to find fingerprints or fibres or anything else at the cottage after all this time, even if you could get in there to search, which you can't. The only other thing would be if Auntie Anne had written something down about the murder – in a diary, say – but Auntie Anne's not that thick. If she *did* commit anything to paper at the time, which is highly unlikely, she'd have destroyed it years ago. So. It'll have to be a confession. But how the heck do you get someone to confess to murder when they know they've got clean away with it? Knowing it'd get her banged up for the rest of her life, why should Auntie Anne admit she pushed her mother? She'd have to be crazy.

'Incredible,' murmured Molly, derailing my train of thought. I looked quizzical and she smiled. 'You may not believe this, Kirsty, but I've lived before too. In the 1920s. I was a boy. A little boy. I drowned, playing near a dam. Fell in and drowned. Nine years old.'

I gazed at her, this person like me, and she was right. I couldn't believe it. It seemed too good to be true.

'How . . . how d'you know you were nine,

Molly, and that it was the Twenties? Where . . .
I mean, I don't get *detail* like that.'

She nodded. 'I know what you mean, love.
I don't dream that clearly either. What
happened was, I was out walking – this was
before my . . . you know? Anyway I was in a
spot I'd never visited before and I came round
a corner and bang – I *knew* the place. There was
a row of cottages and I thought, *That's where
Raymond lived.* Last house in the row. It's white
now, but it was like the others then. *And if I
turn down that narrow lane where the tall chimney
shows over the trees I'll come to the dam.'*

Molly paused and I said, 'And did you?'

'Oh, yes. It was still there. The derelict mill
and its dam.' She shrugged. 'I did some
research. Local rag. I had the address, you see,
and the name. Raymond. All I had to do was
go back through the papers till I found the
story, and I found it. August 1922. Raymond
Lostock, nine. Death by misadventure. Buried
Hathersage cemetery, twenty-second of
August 1922.' She smiled. 'I've even visited
my grave.'

'You haven't?'

She chuckled. 'I have. So you see, you

found the right accomplice. Not through co-incidence of course. I don't believe in coincidence. No. We share a special gift and we found each other. It happens.'

'You mean . . . you'll help me, Molly?'

She grew serious. 'I have no reason to like your aunt, Kirsty. She sacked me the minute my illness started affecting my work, but that's not why I'm on your side. No. I'll do whatever I can because nobody should get away with murder. Trouble is, I'm not all that mobile nowadays. I don't know how . . .'

'You've helped already, Molly. More than you know.' I surprised myself by starting to cry. 'Just to know I'm not the only one. Not barmy. If I can come here sometimes, talk to you.'

'Of course you can, love. Any time. I've been alone too, you know. So alone.' She rose, crossed the space between us without her stick, toppled onto the sofa and wrapped her arms round me. I felt so safe in those arms, so *understood*, I wished I could snuggle for ever.

# Chapter Twenty-three

I got a bus back into town and walked home chanting,

> *Auntie Anne, Auntie Anne,*
> *I'm gonna get you if I can*

inside my head. I don't know where it came from. I certainly hadn't sat on the bus making it up. Maybe Grandma sent it. Anyway, I chanted it all the way home, in time with my footsteps. It was ten to five when I walked into the kitchen. Mum was fussing over a lasagne. 'Where've you been, Kirsty?' she said. 'Anywhere exciting?'

I nodded. 'Library, Mum. There was a shoot-out between bank robbers and librarians. They have it every Tuesday.'

'Really?' She spooned pasta sauce onto a layer of lasagne. 'Remind me to pop down there next week. I like a good shoot-out.'

She's dry, my mum. I wondered whether she'd act so cool if I told her I used to be her mother. I didn't think so. I reminded her she'd be teaching next Tuesday and went up to my room where I could think.

*I'm gonna get you if I can.* Big *if* though, isn't it?

# CHAPTER TWENTY-FOUR

That night I had a dream. So what's new? I hear you cry. Well, it was a different dream for a start. Sort of, anyway.

I was confronting Auntie Anne. We stood face to face and I said, 'Where were you on the afternoon of June 13th 1983?'

'Why? It was before you were born.'

'I know, but it seems so real.'

'Nobody sees the past, dear. It's gone. Dead and gone.'

'A manager at twenty-two, then a murderer. Did you have people under you?'

'I had Molly. Oh, and a woman who cleaned the stairs three evenings a week.'

'Stairs? Which stairs, Auntie Anne?'

'The ones behind you.'

You can probably guess what happened

next. I glanced over my shoulder and saw we were standing at the top of a flight of stairs. Anne lunged forward and shoved me, and I toppled into the same old dream.

Next morning I waited till Dad went upstairs to shave, then said, 'Mum?'

'Yes, dear?' She was sweeping toast crumbs onto a plate with the edge of her hand.

'Did Auntie Anne *know* Grandma Elizabeth meant to change her will?'

Mum glanced up. 'Are you still thinking about *that*, Kirsty?'

'Yes.'

'But *why*, darling? It's ancient history.' She put the plate on the table and scrutinized my features. 'What exactly are you up to?'

I shook my head. 'I'm not up to anything, Mum. I'm interested, that's all.'

'You're a strange child,' she murmured. 'Always have been. But to answer your question – yes, Anne knew. Your grandma was the most open person I ever met. She'd never do anything in a hole-and-corner way. Having decided to alter her will, she sent for Anne and myself and told us.'

'Was Auntie Anne upset?'

'I don't think so. If she was she didn't show it.'

'*I* would've been. I mean, she could've sold the cottage for a lot of money, couldn't she?'

'She *did*, darling, after Grandma's accident. It went to some Arab gentleman with an unprounounceable name. I think your grandma knew Anne would sell the place and she wanted it to stay in the family, and that's why she decided to leave it to your dad and me. We'd have moved in, you see.'

I nodded. 'Hmm. It was sort of – *convenient* for Auntie Anne, wasn't it, Grandma having her accident just then?'

Mum frowned. 'You mustn't talk like that, Kirsty. Anne was devoted to your grandma. She was utterly devastated by the accident. It was weeks before she could hear it mentioned without breaking down. I'm sure she didn't see it as in any way convenient.'

'I'm sorry, Mum. I only meant—'

'I know what you meant, darling, and I didn't mean to snap at you.' She smiled ruefully. 'It has to be said my sister wasted no time disposing of the place, distraught as she was, once she had it, and nobody else ever saw a penny of the proceeds. Still . . .' She smiled again and stood up. 'It's all in the past now. Give me a hand with the dishes, there's a dear.'

All in the past. Dead and gone. That's what Auntie Anne thinks too, but she's mistaken. I'll give her 'utterly devastated' when I work out how to do it. By golly I will.

# CHAPTER TWENTY-FIVE

Frighten her. Spook her. Get her so rattled she loses it completely. Blurts something in front of witnesses.

I was in my room, getting ready to go out. Sally Armitage had phoned. I was meeting her at Island. We'd have Cokes, then check out Our Price and the Body Shop and a few other places. Sally and I were at Cutler's Hill together. She's at Bessamer Comp now but we're still friends.

So here I sit, talking to my reflection in the mirror. Well, I can't talk to anybody else about it, can I? Except Molly, and she's not here.

How d'you spook someone? Well, there's all sorts of ways. I could hang something on Auntie Anne's front door – a white rooster with its throat cut. I saw that in a movie. Or I might make scary phone calls, talking into a hanky to disguise my voice. Then there's anonymous letters. I cocked an eye at the gorgeous creature in the glass. *That'*d be a good one to kick off with, Kirsty. An anonymous letter. Yeah.

We had a nice afternoon, Sally and me. She bought a box of those little coloured balls with bath oil in them, and I got Blur's new single. We chatted quite a bit, but I didn't mention my problem.

It was just after four when I got home. Mum and Dad had been tidying the rockery ready for winter. I went to my room, put Blur on and sat at the computer, trying to compose an anonymous letter. It's hard. Harder than you'd think. You've got to make sure you don't put anything in that might identify you, see? And I wanted it to be scary without being dead obvious. I mean, I didn't want to put, *I know you murdered your mother so admit it, you cow*, or anything like that. No. I was aiming at something a bit more subtle, with a touch of the supernatural. There's nothing like the supernatural for making someone feel uneasy. In the end I came up with this:

*I'm gone, Anne. Dead and gone but I can't rest. And we know why, don't we, you and I? It's our little secret.*

I was dead chuffed with it. I printed it out. One copy. And I *didn't* save it onto disk – I'm not *that* thick. I folded the printout neatly and put it in a very ordinary envelope, which I addressed in block capitals using my left hand. I'd meant to slip out and post it in the box on the corner but I realized I'd have to cadge a stamp off Mum, so instead I hid the thing under the carpet in my room. Tomorrow I'd buy a stamp a mile or two away and post it there. Can't be too careful when you set out to spook a killer.

# CHAPTER TWENTY-SIX

So Thursday morning I left the house with the letter in an inside pocket of my jacket. I bought stamps at the main post office in town and posted it there. I wondered about fingerprints, but since Auntie Anne was hardly going to get the police in I reckoned I was safe. I thought of phoning Molly to let her know what I'd done, but decided to wait and see if my letter had any effect first.

Kids tend to use Island quite a lot and I felt like company, so I checked it out and it must've been my lucky day because Anna Buffham and Kylie Bickerdyke were there. We're not best friends or anything but we're in the same class at school and we get along OK. I got a Coke and walked over.

'Hi, Anna, Kylie. How's things?'

'Great. What you doing here, Kirsty?'

'Messing around.' I sat down. 'How about you?'

'Same. We're off looking at clothes when we've finished these.'

'I'll come with you.' I sipped my Coke. 'Done anything thrilling this week, then?'

'Certainly have,' enthused Kylie. 'I've been to Safeway with my mum – *twice*.'

'Twice!' I gasped. '*And* lived to tell the tale – I wish I had your guts, Kylie.' I looked at Anna. 'How about you?'

Anna leaned forward. 'Listen to this: we went to a garden centre Tuesday. Unarmed. Mum, Dad and me. Near the motorway. We bought bulbs in pots so we'll have hyacinths at Christmas.'

'Hyacinths at *Christmas*?' I goggled. 'Do you realize you can get four *years* for that, you reckless fool?'

'I know, and I don't care.' She eyed me. 'And you. What gut-wrenching stunts have you pulled so far?'

I'd have loved to tell them I was on the trail of a murderer, but of course I couldn't. Instead I leaned forward, cut my eyes this way and that and hissed, 'I posted a letter in broad day-light.'

'Who dares, wins,' murmured Kylie, and Anna laughed with a mouthful of Coke so it came down her nose. It was a daft morning but it took my mind off things. We split up at twelve and I walked home feeling pretty good. Better than Auntie Anne, I thought, when she opens tomorrow's post.

# CHAPTER TWENTY-SEVEN

Well I can't tell you, can I? What happened when Auntie opened her letter, I mean. I wasn't there. We can imagine it though, if you like. Yeah – let's imagine it.

It's breakfast time. Uncle Brian's having kippers, same as always. If you've ever had kippers you'll know how they smell. It's a pong that gets everywhere. You can't get rid of it. Auntie Anne's what they call house-proud – mops and dusts and hoovers and polishes all day long, but you can always smell kippers when you walk in their place. I bet they've had a million rows about it.

Anyway, there they are, the pair of them. Him fiddling with his kippers, her nibbling toast with a sniffy look on her face, and they hear the post. 'Post,' says Anne, and Brian gets

91

up to fetch it. It's just another morning in the life of a successful killer.

There are four items. He fans them out, walking back. There's an appeal from Oxfam, a bill, a business letter for him (he sells car phones) and mine, addressed in block capitals to his wife. 'Just the one for you, dear.' He drops it by her elbow, sits down and starts slitting envelopes with his butter knife.

Anne picks up her envelope, looks at it and frowns. Doesn't recognize the writing. Glances at the postmark. Yaxley. Somebody local then. She opens the envelope, extracts the neatly folded note, smooths it out, reads.

*I'm gone, Anne. Dead and gone but I can't rest. And we know why, don't we, you and I? It's our little secret.*

A small noise – a sharp intake of breath per-haps – causes Brian to look up. 'Something the matter?'

Anne swallows, shakes her head. 'No, no. Touched the cafetière with the back of my hand, that's all. Hot.'

'Hmm.' He goes back to his letter. Anne, heart pounding, reads the note again more slowly but there's no mistake. It reads as it did the first time, and there's no doubt in her mind what it's about. She refolds the thin paper, inhaling slowly in the hope that this might calm her, but her hands tremble as she returns the note to its envelope and slips it into the pocket of her smock. She can inhale slowly till she's blue in the face but it'll be a long, long time before Auntie Anne feels calm again. Her niece will see to that.

And her mother.

# CHAPTER TWENTY-EIGHT

As it turned out, Auntie Anne wasn't the only one to get a shock that Friday morning. I came down to breakfast with a video playing inside my head of Anne opening my letter, and Mum said, 'Your dad and I have to be in school today, Kirsty. You know – setting up for the new half term, so I've phoned Auntie Anne and she'll do you some lunch.'

Terrific. Spook a killer, then go have lunch with her. I protested, trying to keep my voice from shaking. 'We don't need to bother Auntie Anne, Mum. I'm thirteen. I can get my own lunch.'

Mum shook her head. 'That's not the point, dear. We don't like the idea of leaving you in the house all day on your own. I *know* you think of yourself as grown up, but thirteen's not really that old, and you hear of such awful things happening these days. Your father and I will feel easier in our minds if we know some-one's keeping an eye on you.'

Yeah, right. I know what you mean, Mum. *I'd* feel much better knowing my kid was hav-ing lunch with someone who murdered her own mother. I didn't say this of course. I said, 'But Mum . . .'

'Kirsty!' Dad gazed at me over the top of his specs. 'Don't argue with your mother, please. Your aunt expects you at eleven o'clock, and you'll be there. Is that clear?'

I sighed. 'Yes, Dad.' It's terrific, having teachers for parents. Like being at a boarding school where there are no holidays.

'And don't be bothering Anne with your questions about Grandma Elizabeth,' put in Mum. 'She still gets upset.'

Yes, I thought but didn't say, and she's going to get a whole lot upsetter before I'm through.

So. I'd be arriving at my auntie's about three hours after my letter. Hairy end to half-term, or what?

# CHAPTER TWENTY-NINE

I was dead nervous walking round to my auntie's. What if I hadn't been careful enough and she knew I sent the note? Or if she didn't know but mentioned it to me – would I blush and give myself away? I wished something would happen that'd give me an excuse not to go. A slight accident. Joe showing up for an unexpected visit. The start of World War Three.

Naturally none of these things happened, and at eleven o'clock precisely I knocked on the murderer's door.

'Come on in, dear – you're right on time.' She didn't sound delighted – tired would be nearer the mark. I followed her through, looking on every flat surface for my note. Needless to say it was nowhere in sight. In the spotless lounge she said, 'Lunch will be at half past twelve, dear. Would you like some coffee?'

'Uh – yes please, Auntie Anne.' I sat down, hoping I didn't look as nervous as I felt.

She brought a tray through and sat in the other chair. I watched her pour, looking for signs of tension. I didn't spot any. It was ten past eleven. I wondered what the heck we'd find to talk about till half twelve.

'Have you thought any more about a career, Kirsty?'

'Uh? Oh, no. No – I've decided not to bother till I'm about fifteen.'

'Absolutely right. Childhood's to be enjoyed, and it passes so very quickly. Have you heard from your brother lately?'

'Joe? No. He's not a letter writer. Mum watches the post, but she's nearly always disappointed.'

'Well.' Anne sipped her coffee. 'They say no news is good news.'

'Oh yes.' I nodded, looking at her over the rim of my cup. 'Better no letter at all than one with something bad in it.'

Something in her face. A flicker. I took a ginger biscuit. Nibbled. Anne's cup chattered a bit in its saucer. I looked across. Her hands were quivering ever so slightly. She saw I'd noticed and smiled ruefully. 'Nerves. Never give in to your nerves, Kirsty. I did. They've ruled me all my life.'

'I get twitchy too when something upsets me.' I smiled. 'It must be in the genes.' I looked at her. 'Are you upset about something, Auntie Anne?'

'Me? No. No – I'm a martyr to my nerves, that's all.'

I chuckled. 'Martyr. Funny – that's the second time I've heard that word today. Mum said *her* mother was a martyr to rheumatism.'

'Oh . . . did she? How did that come up, Kirsty?'

I shrugged. 'Mum felt a twinge, I think. She reckons it's hereditary.'

'Yes, well . . . I believe it is. And it's certainly true your grandma suffered with it. In fact it killed her, really.'

'Did it?' I gazed across at her. 'I thought it was a fall, Auntie Anne. Down some stairs.'

'Yes dear, it *was*, but you see the rheumatism made her unsteady on her feet and that's *why* she fell.'

'Ah.' I popped the last bit of biscuit in my mouth and chewed. 'What a sad way to die, Auntie Anne. Can't help your nerves much, thinking about that.'

'I – try *not* to think about it, Kirsty.'

I just bet you do, I thought. I didn't *say* it, of course. I just nodded, and a minute later she mumbled something about potatoes and went out to the kitchen. I stayed where I was, sipping coffee and feeling chuffed with myself. My Spook-Auntie-Anne campaign seemed to have got off to a promising start, *and* we were having steak and kidney pie for lunch.

I wonder if they get steak and kidney pie in prison?

# CHAPTER THIRTY

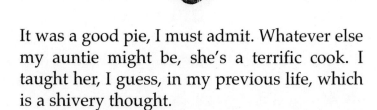

It was a good pie, I must admit. Whatever else my auntie might be, she's a terrific cook. I taught her, I guess, in my previous life, which is a shivery thought.

We didn't talk much over lunch. We never do. As I said before, I can't stand her and she senses it. Anyway, she'd be busy with her thoughts. I know *I* was.

*OK, Sherlock – this was the first move. What's the second? She's rattled, but not to where she's about to confess. The thing to do is keep her reeling – give her no time to recover. But how?*

Inspiration struck over pudding, only it wasn't inspiration so much as a sort of vision. There's this vase on Auntie Anne's sideboard. An art deco vase from the Twenties in yellow, green and red. It's been there years, but as my vacant stare alighted on it that lunchtime, I saw it somewhere else. I saw it on dusty floorboards in a dim place that was crammed with junk. It only lasted a second, and as it faded I heard myself say, 'Why on *earth* did you rescue that horrid old thing from the Glory Hole, Anne?'

It wasn't me speaking. It wasn't. I wouldn't have dared call anything of Auntie Anne's horrid, especially in the circumstances. The words came out of my mouth but I wasn't responsible for them.

'What?' She paused, a forkful of glazed pear halfway to her lips. 'What was that you said, Kirsty?'

'N-nothing, Auntie Anne. I was – day-dreaming.'

She set down her fork. 'No you weren't. You said something about my vase. Something rude. And you mentioned . . . you said, "the Glory Hole". Sylvia – your mother – she's been talking about it, hasn't she? About the Glory Hole? What was she doing, eh? Sneering? About my lack of taste – was *that* it?'

'No!' I shook my head. I could see she was blazing mad and I was really scared. 'Nobody's been sneering, Auntie Anne. Honestly. Not Mum. Not anybody. Why *should* they?'

'*Somebody*'s talked to you, Kirsty, or you wouldn't know about the Glory Hole, or that the vase was up there.'

'I . . . can't explain. I had a sort of daydream, that's all. I saw the vase on the floor. I *saw* it.' I could hardly get the words round the lump in my throat, and when I saw she didn't believe me I burst into tears.

She didn't comfort me. She wouldn't have, even if she'd not been mad. It isn't her way. She picked up her fork and set about demolishing her pear, leaving me to recover as best I might. The only good thing was, when I'd got a grip on myself and blown my nose and dabbed my eyes and all that, she didn't resume her interrogation, but we spent a ghastly afternoon all the same. I was glad when three o'clock crawled round and Dad showed up to drive me home.

Oh – there was one other good thing. All the time Auntie Anne was eating her pudding, her fork hand was shaking like mad.

# CHAPTER THIRTY-ONE

She phoned Mum. She did. I couldn't believe it. I mean, I'd have thought she'd want to keep the whole thing quiet, but no. At eight that night I was in my room listening to music when Mum stuck her head round the door and motioned me to turn down the volume. I thought the noise was bugging her, but it wasn't that.

'I've had your auntie on the phone,' she said. 'What happened at lunchtime, Kirsty? Anne tells me you made a remark about a vase. A rude remark. She practically accused me of talking to you about her behind her back.'

I shook my head. 'I wasn't rude, Mum. Not on purpose. I tried to explain to Auntie Anne but she wouldn't believe me.'

'Well.' Mum sat down on the bed. 'I think you'd better tell me what you told her, young woman.'

So I did, and she didn't believe me either. 'You *saw* the vase on the floor in Grandma's loft – is that what you're saying?'

I nodded.

'But how? How is that possible, Kirsty? How can anybody see something that happened years ago, before they were born?'

I shrugged. 'I don't know, Mum. All I know is that I did. I – get things like that now and then.' I pulled the chair away from the dressing table and sat facing her.

Mum nodded, frowning. 'I know. You mentioned the Glory Hole once when you were about seven. I asked you who'd talked to you about Grandma's attic and you said nobody. And once, when you were a baby, you pointed to your grandad in the snapshot on the sideboard and said "Bob", which was his name, though you couldn't possibly have known that then. You said it twice.' She shook her head. 'I don't know, Kirsty. Really I don't. You're a strange child.'

'I know I am.' Well – what *else* could I say,

short of blabbing the whole reincarnation thing?

Mum sighed. 'Well anyway, you must apologize to your auntie, Kirsty. Write her a note if you feel you can't face her, and let me see it before you seal the envelope.' She stood up. 'There's more than enough unhappiness in the world without families falling out.'

She was right of course. There is, but I couldn't see Auntie Anne being appeased by a written apology from me. Especially if it came on the same paper as that other note.

Hey, *that*'s an idea. I could make it part of my Spook-Auntie-Anne campaign.

# CHAPTER THIRTY-TWO

I had a long think, then wrote this:

*Dear Auntie Anne,*

*I'm writing to apologize for my behaviour on Friday. I didn't mean to call your vase horrid. It isn't horrid. In fact I've always liked it. I know I was rude, but I didn't lie to you. I do sometimes get funny turns when I seem to see bits of the past: you might remember the incident in Mr Newell's class I once told you about. I see other things too, most of them not very nice. So I really did see your vase on dusty floorboards but I shouldn't have said what I said, and I'm sorry. I hope you can forgive me.*

*Love,*
*Kirsty*

I did it on the PC, printed it out and took it to Mum. She read it and looked at me. '*What* incident in Mr Newell's class, dear?'

'Tell you later, Mum. I can catch the last collection if I'm quick.' I hoped she might forget in the meantime. I used an envelope from the same pack, but this time I addressed it in my normal writing using my right hand. It was the same ballpoint though, and I *did* catch the collection, so my auntie would get it in the morning.

# CHAPTER THIRTY-THREE

Next day was Saturday. Sally and I had fixed to meet at half ten at the coffee shop. I'd had my breakfast and was in my room getting ready when the phone rang and Dad yelled, 'Kirsty – phone!' I thought it was Sally to say she couldn't make it, but as he passed me the handset Dad whispered, 'Your Auntie Anne.'

I nearly died. I'd just been thinking about her. I swallowed and croaked, 'Auntie Anne?'

'Ah, Kirsty. I have your note. Thank you.'

'That's OK. I hope . . .'

'The thing is, it looks suspiciously similar to a note I received yesterday. Did you write that one as well, Kirsty?'

'No Auntie Anne, I didn't. I've only written the one, honestly. What was the other about?'

'Never you mind. Do your parents know about these – funny turns you mention?'

'No. Not really. I don't like to mention them in case they think I'm barmy. They know about the dream though, because I used to wake up screaming.'

'Dream? What dream, Kirsty?'

'This dream I've had since I was small. It's a nightmare. I'm at the top of some dark stairs and . . . something makes me fall. It's horrible.'

A silence followed this. I could almost *see* the colour draining from her cheeks. It was brilliant. After a bit she said, 'Yes, it must be absolutely dreadful. Do you . . . still get it?'

'Sometimes, but I don't scream any more. I guess I've got used to it.'

'Yes, but still . . . Anyway.' She injected some briskness into her voice. 'If you're absolutely sure you didn't write this other note, we'll say no more about it. Goodbye, Kirsty. Give my regards to your mum.'

'I will. 'Bye, Auntie Anne. And thanks.'

Bit of an abrupt end to our little talk but then she'd a lot to think about, and she wasn't the only one.

109

# CHAPTER THIRTY-FOUR

I met Sally and we did the usual stuff. It didn't feel quite as good as last time because half-term was nearly over. 'School Monday,' she murmured, as we checked out the new singles at Our Price.

'Oooh, don't,' I moaned. 'Makes me poorly just thinking about it. Still . . .' I brightened a fraction, remembering. 'There's the Hallowe'en Rave to look forward to.' School was putting on this rave on the 31st, six-thirty till nine-thirty. They have it every year. It's the only good thing about Fettler's.

'Huh – all right for some. We never have owt like that up Bessamer. They don't know what a rave *is* at that dump.'

I chuckled. 'Talk to my dad. Maybe he'll run one.'

'Oh yeah – I can just see it.'

'Well – you should've come to Fettler's, same as me.'

'Didn't get the option, you turkey. Mum went to Bessamer so *I* had to go. Dunno why – it didn't exactly make a genius out of *her*.' She clucked disgustedly. 'Parents.'

I had a dream that night, and it wasn't my nightmare. There were two little girls in this dream. Sisters, seven or eight years old. One of them was heartbroken because the other had pinched her Barbie doll and sold it to some kid for a shilling. I was telling her off, really shouting, trying to make her cry but all she did was look back at me with an impudent expression, saying, 'Parents,' over and over in a scornful voice. As I yelled at her she spun the coin and caught it on the back of her left hand. 'Heads I win,' she murmured, 'tails you lose.' I was furious and tried to grab hold of her but I couldn't move. She turned away slowly, smiling, and that's when I woke up.

I know what you're thinking. The two little girls were Mum and Auntie Anne, right? Well that's what *I* thought, but the question was this: was it something that *really* happened – another of my flashbacks – or was it just a dream? I'd no idea, but what I did was write it down in my notebook, because if it *was* a glimpse into the past it might come in very handy for my Spook-Auntie-Anne campaign.

If I'd stopped to think, I might have realized the game I was playing was growing more deadly every day, but I didn't. I was too absorbed. If I'd been able to see into the near future as well as the distant past, I think I'd have dropped the whole thing.

# CHAPTER THIRTY-FIVE

When it's wet I'm always dead early for school, because either Mum or Dad'll drop me off and they like to be at work by half eight. It was wet that Monday morning after the October break. I said goodbye to Mum and ran across the yard with my blazer over my head making for the covered area, and when I got there I had it to myself.

It was eight fifteen. I leaned on a pillar, watching raindrops falling like a bead curtain from the edge of the roof. A teacher's car came nosing through the gateway and swished by on its way to the parking area behind the main block, with old Baldock at the wheel. She's a Christian. Teaches RE. A sixth former told me she tries every year to get the Hallowe'en Rave stopped on the grounds that it's unchristian, yet she'll happily celebrate Diwali, Eid, Chanukah and Wesak. I wondered how she'd be on reincarnation.

Kids started drifting in at twenty-five past. Kylie Bickerdyke was on her bike as always. She parked it and came over. 'Hi, Kirsty. Great to be back, or what?' Rain beaded her glasses, made rat-tails of her hair.

'What,' I growled, and we laughed. She produced a crumpled Kleenex, whipped off her specs and started polishing them. A minute later Anna Buffham showed up. Her dad always dropped her off. 'Hi, Kylie, Kirsty. Good half-term?'

Kylie rehung her glasses and blinked at her friend. 'Not long enough. Roll on flippin' Christmas, I say.'

Anna nodded. 'Absolutely.'

'Baldock's abolishing it,' I told them. 'Unpagan.' That got a laugh, but actually I didn't feel like joking. Couldn't stop brooding over the Auntie Anne business. I'd started something that I had to finish somehow, but how? And when? Would it be over by Christmas, and if it was, what sort of Christmas would it be, with my auntie in jail and me responsible? Would Mum hate me? Anne was her sister, after all. And what about the other thing – me being Mum's mother? *That*'ll all come out, won't it? Bound to. And what then? Can it ever be the same between Mum and me? Can't see how. And the rotten thing is, I can't even talk to my friends about it.

There was one person I *could* talk to, though. Molly. I'd call her, lunchtime. From the box outside school. Fix to go see her. The buzzer sounded and I moved forward, merging with the throng, wishing I was one of them and one of them was me.

# CHAPTER THIRTY-SIX

I got a surprise, lunchtime. More of a shock really. I'd scoffed my sandwich, slurped my juice and was dashing through the gateway to phone when somebody tooted a horn. I looked across and there was Auntie Anne's red Polo with its window down and Nefertiti herself eyeballing me. I nearly died. She didn't smile or call out or anything but sat looking while I restarted my heart and trogged across, trying to look normal.

'Auntie Anne . . . what're *you* doing here?' Well – I had to say something, didn't I?

'I came hoping to see *you*, Kirsty. I expected to have to ask somebody to fetch you, but here you are. Where were you going, by the way?'

'Er – phone, Auntie Anne. I have to make a phone call.'

'Ah. Some boy, I suppose.' She still wasn't smiling. 'Well, never mind that now. Come round, get in. I want to show you something.'

My heart was battering my ribcage like it was trying to get out. I walked round the Polo. She leaned across, opened the door. I slid in.

'Look.' She thrust a sheet of paper at me. I took it, smoothed it in my lap. It was my note, but the first bit had been obliterated with Tipp-Ex. Now it read, *And we know why, don't we, you and I? It's our little secret.*

I swallowed, feeling my cheeks burn. 'Is this the other note you mentioned, Auntie Anne?' I knew it was, of course. God, was I scared.

'It certainly is. And now look.' She waved a second sheet in my face. It was my apology. 'Notice the similarities. Same paper, same spacing, same margins, same figure one at the foot. Same PC, I'd say.'

'No.' I shook my head again. 'This isn't mine, Auntie Anne. I told you – I only sent the one. I don't even know what this one *means*. And anyway it's been Tipp-Exed. I don't have Tipp-Ex.'

She scoffed. '*I* obliterated that line, Kirsty,

117

because it referred to something . . . personal. Highly personal. I think you wrote both notes.'

'But Auntie Anne – if I'd written this one I'd *know* what the first line said, wouldn't I? There'd be no point painting it out.' I reckoned that was pretty good, considering I was practically wetting my pants with terror.

She snorted. 'Very good, Kirsty. Very smart.' She jerked the note from my hand, screwed it up and shoved it in her bag. 'You don't fool me for one minute, girl, so don't think it. You're a child. A profoundly *disturbed* child if you ask me. You think you know something but you know nothing. Nothing.' She leaned across me and opened the door. 'Go make your phone call, and don't write me any more notes or I'll speak to your parents about getting help for you. Psychiatric help.'

I got out fast, I can tell you. Afterwards I wished I'd said something. Some parting shot, like, *It's* you *needs a shrink, Auntie Anne. A* prison *shrink maybe*, but I couldn't think of anything at the time, I was so rattled. I walked off shaking and after a minute she roared past, eyes front. If I'd needed to talk to Molly before, I certainly did now. By golly I did.

# CHAPTER THIRTY-SEVEN

'Molly?'

'Yes . . . who's speaking?'

'It's me, Kirsty.'

'Oh – oh yes of course. How are you, Kirsty?'

'Not so good, Molly. That's why I'm calling. I'm . . . all mixed up. Don't know what to do.'

'Why, dear – has something happened?'

'No. Well . . . yes, a couple of things, but it isn't that. I just don't know whether I can . . . you know – turn my auntie in.'

'Hmm. Well Kirsty, I can't make that decision for you. It's really a family matter and I'm an outsider, but I will say this: to know a crime's been committed and not tell the police is a serious offence, even if the criminal is a relative. In other circumstances I'd say you had no choice, but since your suspicion arises out of dreams and memories of a previous life, you could remain silent on the grounds that it might all be nonsense, or that nobody would believe you if you *did* tell.'

'Yes.' Through the streaky glass wall of the phone box I could see kids trooping back to school. It was twenty to two. 'But you see, Molly, I'm *sure*. Absolutely sure. If I wasn't, I wouldn't have come to you in the first place. And there's something else.'

'I *thought* there was, because you're sounding distinctly shaky. You'd better tell me.'

'Well . . . I sent my auntie a note. An anonymous note. I was really careful, but she's linked it up with some other stuff . . . things I said, another note . . . and now she suspects me. She was here just now, outside school, waiting for me. I'm scared, Molly.'

'Hmm . . . dodgy, I'll admit. Well look – we can't really sort this out over the phone, Kirsty. Why don't you come up and see me – this evening if you're not too busy. And in the meantime I'll have a think and see if I can't come up with something that'll help. What d'you say?'

'I . . . yes, I'll come. I don't know what time exactly, but I'll come tonight. And thanks, Molly. I mean it.'

'I know you do, dear. I'll see you soon, then. 'Bye.'

''Bye, Molly.'

I hung up and walked back to school feeling a bit better. Only a bit, mind.

# CHAPTER THIRTY-EIGHT

Molly gazed at me from her armchair. 'You're trying to make your aunt believe her mother's come back from the *grave*?'

'Yes. I thought that'd be the best way to make her confess. You know – scare her half to death.'

'Hmm.' She shook her head. 'As I recall, your aunt's the down-to-earth sort. Not the type to believe in ghosts, I wouldn't have thought. Still.' She sighed. 'You've started that way, so I suppose we're stuck with it. Well, all right. Look, why don't we fix it so your aunt gets an anonymous phone call from her mother when you're actually in her house? *That*'ll throw her off the scent, won't it?'

I looked at her. 'Well yes, it'd be absolutely

terrific, but why would I go to her house? I never go unless I have to.'

Molly smiled. 'Pretend you came to protest your innocence. We'll fix a time, and you knock on her door the very moment I'm reciting this little rhyme:

> *June thirteenth of '83.*
> *I didn't see you, but you saw me.'*

I gazed at her. 'That's *brilliant*, Molly, but it'll need exact timing. And what if Uncle Brian picks up?'

'I thought of that. If your uncle picks up I ask for Anne. If he says Anne's out I say, *When she gets back, recite this rhyme to her. She'll know who it was calling.* Then I say the rhyme. Whatever happens I'll be speaking as you're knocking. All we have to do is synchronize our watches. We'll do it *now*, this evening, if you like.'

And that's how I found myself creeping up a killer's path at one minute to nine on a dark, drizzly evening with my heart in my mouth, praying for the sound of a phone.

# CHAPTER THIRTY-NINE

I loitered by the front door. There's a little panel of rippled glass in it. No light showed through the glass so the hallway, where the phone stood on a small table, was in darkness. I tried to look at my watch but there wasn't enough light. 'Come on, Molly,' I whispered. 'For Pete's sake come *on*.'

I nearly chickened out. I did. I was about three seconds away from scurrying down the path when the phone rang. God, talk about jump. I nearly died. Light showed through the glass as somebody opened a door inside, then the hall light came on and the ringing stopped and I heard Uncle Brian's voice. I took a deep breath and knocked.

'Anne!' I heard him call my aunt, and a second later his face appeared, distorted by the glass. I just had time to think, *Does he know about any of this – has Auntie Anne told him?* and then the door opened and there he was.

'Kirsty, at *this* time of night! It's after nine.'

'I know. I wanted a word with Auntie Anne.' I looked past him. She was standing with the handset to her ear, staring at me while she listened to Molly. You should have seen her face. 'I can see she's busy though. It'll do tomorrow.' Boy, did I want out of there! We'd fouled up, you see, Molly and me. Hadn't considered whether my uncle shared his wife's secret. It was crucial, I could see that now. If he knew nothing and I mentioned our lunchtime encounter in front of him, he was going to want to know what the heck it was all about. And if he *was* in on it, there'd be *two* of them after me instead of one.

'No, no.' He shook his head and stepped aside. 'Come on in, love. Your auntie won't be a minute.' He smiled. 'Can't be turning you away, can we, when you've come specially. What *would* you think of us, eh?'

I smiled and stepped inside because I had no choice. A line from a nursery rhyme went through my head as I followed him past my auntie and into the living room. *Won't you step into my parlour? said the spider to the fly.* It didn't help, I can tell you. I was like that fly, only worse.

*Two* spiders.

# CHAPTER FORTY

'Tea, coffee?'

'Oh – coffee, please. No sugar.'

He smiled. 'Not watching your weight, surely. Not at thirteen.'

'Save me watching it later.' If there *is* any later, I added, but to myself.

'True.' He left the room as my auntie came in, looking pale. 'Not a word about ... you know,' she murmured, lowering herself into the armchair opposite mine, 'our little talk earlier. Your uncle knows nothing about it and I don't want him to.' She kept her voice low and an eye on the doorway. 'I – it seems I owe you an apology, Kirsty. I know now the note wasn't from you.'

I nodded. 'That's what I came to tell you,

127

Auntie Anne. That it wasn't from me.' I looked at her. 'How d'you . . . ?'

'Never mind. Your uncle's coming. So.' She adjusted her volume control as he appeared behind a loaded tray. 'You've decided university might be a better idea than plunging straight into the world of work, eh? I think you're very wise.' She looked at Uncle Brian as he set down the tray. 'Don't you think she's wise, darling?'

My uncle nodded. 'I'm sure she is, my dear.' He grinned ruefully. 'What I *don't* understand is why our wise niece felt compelled to communicate her decision to you at nine o'clock at night when it'll be – what – five years before she actually starts university.' He was joking, but my auntie explained anyway.

'Ah, well, you see, Kirsty came to see me the other day about her future.' She chuckled. 'Apparently they start asking pretty early on at school what their pupils want to do with their lives. Anyway we talked, and I suppose I must have put Kirsty off the idea of work at sixteen, hence her decision. Anyway, nine o'clock's not *that* late. The poor girl'll think she's not welcome if you keep going on about the time.'

'No no!' He shook his head. 'I didn't mean . . .' He looked at me. 'You know I didn't mean *that*, don't you, Kirsty? You're welcome any time at this house. Any time at all.'

I nodded, wanting only to be gone. 'I know, and I wouldn't have come, only I was passing on my way home and I thought . . .'

He nodded. 'Quite right too. Ignore the geriatric grousings of your miserable old uncle and drink your coffee while it's hot.' He turned to Auntie Anne. 'Who was that on the phone, by the way? Didn't recognize the voice.'

'Pooh! Some woman selling insurance, that's all. Damned cheek. I let her rattle on a bit, then hung up without speaking. Only way to deal with that sort of thing.'

Smooth liar under pressure, my Auntie Anne. Takes after her 'mother', you might say.

# CHAPTER FORTY-ONE

So Molly's plan worked perfectly: my auntie thinks her dead mother's composing when she should be *de*composing and I'm in the clear, right?

Well, I dunno. She's vain and snobby and she murdered her own mother, but Auntie Anne's not thick. It'd be dangerous to underestimate her.

I'd learned one interesting thing though. Uncle Brian wasn't in on his wife's dark secret. I couldn't decide whether that was going to make things easier or harder.

'And where have you been, young woman?' goes Dad. Head of English and he starts a sentence with 'And'.

'Sally's.'

'Till *this* time?'

'No, Dad. Till a quarter of an hour ago, then there's the walk home.'

'Yes, and that's the bit your mother and I don't like, Kirsty. The walk home. Have you any idea how many young women are murdered, walking home?'

'No, Dad. Have you?'

'Too many, that's how many. Nine o'clock's far too late for a girl to be out alone. In future we want you to phone if you're going to be late, and one of us will come and pick you up.'

Great. I *told* you it's wonderful having teachers for parents, didn't I? Anyway, I didn't argue. I'd just had a brill idea for my next note and I couldn't wait to try it out.

# CHAPTER FORTY-TWO

I've got this disk. This encyclopaedia. If you enter MUMMY a picture comes on screen of an Egyptian mummy in a golden casket. It's a diagram showing three views of the casket – front, back and side. I got it on screen, took a printout, circled the back view in red crayon and wrote the words MUMMY'S BACK underneath. *MUMMY'S BACK*. Geddit?

I folded the printout, shoved it in an envelope and addressed it to Auntie Anne. I could hardly write for giggling. MUMMY'S BACK. You've got to admit it's *really* funny. I had stamps left from when I posted the first note, so I stuck one on and hid the envelope in the bag I use for school.

I'd just finished when I remembered the dream I'd had about the two little girls.

Remember? One had sold the other's doll, but I had no way of knowing whether it really happened? Well, I decided to take a chance. Trust my dream. After all, my dreams had proved pretty accurate up to now and the computer was on, so I might as well do a note. I wrote this:

*Remember when you sold your sister's doll, Anne? I do. I ought to have known then you were far too fond of money.*

I printed it out and closed straight away without saving. Wouldn't do for Mum to walk in and see *that* on screen. Another envelope, another stamp, and then all I had to decide was which to post first, doll or mummy.

No contest.

# CHAPTER FORTY-THREE

I dreamed a scary dream. Not the stairs. That one wasn't coming much any more. In this dream it was night and I was walking in a dark, lonely place. There were buildings of some sort but nobody was in them, and there were like high hedges on both sides which I couldn't see over. There was a glow in the sky ahead of me and I was walking towards it, but it was quite far away. I was trying to hurry – I was frightened – but something loose I was wearing kept catching on the hedge and I had to keep stopping to free myself. I'd just done this for the umpteenth time when a figure stepped out of the bushes in front of me. It was silhouetted against the glow so I couldn't see its face. I didn't recognize the person but there was an overwhelming sense of menace, and as whoever it was drew near I screamed and woke up. My heart was thumping like mad and it was ages before I nodded off again.

I posted MUMMY'S BACK next morning on my way to school. It wasn't raining so I walked, taking the short cut through the allotments which brings you out on the school's all-weather pitch. We're not supposed to come that way – there's a school rule against it, plus the allotment holders don't like it, but it cuts off a big corner and gets you away from the traffic. Loads of kids use it.

It was an ordinary Tuesday at school. All the routine stuff, but I managed to liven it up for myself by imagining the postman emptying the box, dropping my envelope in his bag, and Auntie Anne opening it tomorrow morning. It'd certainly take her mind off the smell of kippers for a minute or two.

# CHAPTER FORTY-FOUR

First period Wednesday morning we had RE with old Baldock. We were doing the spread of Buddhism, and Baldock was explaining how bits of earlier religions got mixed in with Buddhism as it spread, altering it in various ways so that now there were various schools of Buddhism, though they all had the same basic beliefs.

'Something similar happened to Christianity,' she said, 'as it seeped into northern Europe, so that we celebrate Easter with decorated eggs and Christmas with mistletoe, holly and other evergreen boughs. These are remnants of paganism, sometimes called the "old religion".'

'What about Hallowe'en, Miss?' This from Anthony Yallop, the class clown. Everybody knew how old Baldock felt about Hallowe'en. With a bit of luck Anthony's question would divert her till the buzzer.

'Hallowe'en.' She said it like you might say 'Doggy poo' – distaste warping her mouth. 'Hallowe'en actually means holy evening, Anthony. It's the eve of All Hallows, or All Saints' Day, but it falls on the same day as an earlier, pagan festival to do with witches and hobgoblins and so forth and its Christian significance is now buried under a commercially generated avalanche of the symbols of gross superstition.'

'Yeah, but like,' pursued Anthony, 'it means that when we have the Hallowe'en Rave a week tomorrow we'll *really* be celebrating a Christian festival?'

Baldock shook her head. 'Not dolled up as witches and warlocks you won't. Not with pumpkin lanterns and broomsticks and masks. Not with bats and cats and spiders and whatnot. Nothing remotely Christian about any of that, I can assure you.'

'But, Miss . . .' The boy puckered his brow. 'If it's OK to have Easter eggs, and Christmas trees and all that even though *they*'re pagan, what's wrong with having pagan stuff at Hallowe'en? I don't get it.'

He did a great job, old Yallop. Kept Baldock busy for twenty-five minutes and wound her up into the bargain. As a practising Christian she's supposed to be gentle and mild but you could see her struggling to control herself. It was brilliant. Three hundred years ago she'd have burned him at the stake.

It was breaktime before I remembered Auntie Anne. MUMMY'S BACK. Gross superstition of course, but all the same it'd prey on her mind, and I'd be slipping along to the postbox with my second note at lunchtime. Talk about piling it on.

# CHAPTER FORTY-FIVE

Walking back from the postbox I decided it was time I phoned Molly. She'd be waiting to hear how her plan had worked Monday night, and I wanted her to know about my latest notes. I made a detour that afternoon and called her from the library.

'Molly?'

'Kirsty. Are you all right? I've been worried.'

'Sorry. I guess I should have called yesterday. I'm fine. Your plan worked like magic. Auntie Anne looked as if she'd seen a ghost, and she actually apologized for having suspected me.'

'That's good. You *will* be careful though, dear, won't you? It's a dangerous game we're playing.'

'I know, Molly, and I *am* being careful. I've posted two more notes.' I told her about them. She chuckled over MUMMY'S BACK but thought the other a bit dodgy. 'What if your dream wasn't about Anne, Kirsty? What if it wasn't about real people at all?'

'Well,' I countered, 'if it wasn't about her she'll be mystified. Maybe she'll think she *did* sell Mum's doll but that she's forgotten. Anyway,' I smiled, 'you've got to admit my dreams have been pretty reliable up to now, which reminds me.'

I told her about last night's dream and she said, 'Well, Kirsty, I hope that's *one* that doesn't come true.'

I laughed. 'No chance, Molly. That one *was* just a dream.'

Neither of my parents was home when I got in, so I didn't have to explain why I was late. I peeled some spuds and got green beans and pizzas from the freezer. We eat a lot of convenience foods at our house, especially when I'm first home. When I'd got everything started I went up to my room to work on my witch's outfit for the Hallowe'en Rave. I'd cadged three metres of fine black nylon net from Grandma Kath. There's a prize for the best costume, and this year it's going to be mine.

# CHAPTER FORTY-SIX

I *am* being careful. That's what I'd told Molly, but I hadn't been careful enough. As I sat on the bed putting lace and satin together to make a witch's dress, Auntie Anne was busy putting two and two together to make four, though of course I didn't know this at the time.

It was the stamps. I'd bought a book of four the day I posted the first note. You know – *I'm gone, Anne.* That one. I'd used two of the stamps on that and my note of apology, and the other two on MUMMY'S BACK and the doll note, but in tearing out the second stamp I'd been careless. I didn't notice at the time that it hadn't torn cleanly along the perforation but had lost a corner. It was just a tiny corner, left attached to the next stamp, but I'd stuck that one on MUMMY'S BACK, so Auntie Anne ended up with both stamps. Now I've said she wasn't thick and she wasn't. She'd hung on to the envelope with the incomplete stamp, and when she got the one with the extra bit she compared them. The extra bit on MUMMY'S BACK fitted exactly the missing corner on my apology and bingo! She had me cold.

If I'd known, I wouldn't have sat there sewing a flipping witch outfit, I can tell you. What I can't tell you is what I'd have done instead. Died, probably.

# CHAPTER FORTY-SEVEN

I don't know what I expected my two notes to do, but whatever it was I was doomed to disappointment. Nothing happened at all. Or perhaps I should say nothing *seemed* to happen. In fact, having proved herself a better detective than I was, Auntie Anne was planning a showdown, but that's for later. In the meantime my life went on as normal, or as near normal as it has ever been.

Thursday, the talk at school was all about the Hallowe'en Rave, now a week away. Anthony Yallop claimed he intended coming as Irene Baldock, complete with cross and Bible. 'I'll be by the door,' he told us, 'cursing all you sad pagan plonkers as you go in.'

'You wouldn't dare,' taunted Kylie. 'Old Swanny'd suspend you for a month or expel you, and anyway you couldn't make the costume. Boys' costumes are always rubbish.'

'Not this one,' rejoined Anthony. 'It's a dress my gran wore about seventy years ago so it's just like the stuff Baldock trolls around in. Only one snag – I'm too good-looking.'

'Hooo!' cried Maureen Crossley. 'You're about as good-looking as a bagful of chisels, you tube. In fact if I had to choose, I'd go for the chisels every time.'

There was more like that. Everybody was making an outfit. Everybody hoped to take the prize, which this year was a CD ROM software package. I kept quiet about my own effort, which I believed was good enough to win.

Sally phoned at teatime, inviting me round. The wrinklies let me go by myself but Dad insisted on picking me up after. It was a good evening. We talked and listened to music and Sally's mum sent out for a pizza. I didn't mention the rave because I knew Sally envied us Fettler's kids, and at half nine Dad showed up to drive me home. Sally stood on the step, waving. I waved back, blissfully ignorant of the awful thing that was to happen before I'd see her again.

# CHAPTER FORTY-EIGHT

So that was Thursday. Friday slipped by, then Saturday, without a murmur from Auntie Anne. It was sort of spooky, waiting for something to happen. Wondering how long I should give it before trying something else.

To be absolutely honest I was getting fed up with the whole thing. I mean, excitement's OK in small doses but it starts to get to you after a while. You're tense all the time. Can't relax. You know – have I given myself away? What if she's waiting when I come out of school? What if she's phoned Mum? Molly's warning kept replaying inside my skull: *It's a dangerous game we're playing.*

A dangerous game, yes, and one I couldn't just choose to abandon. You know about a murder, I kept telling myself. A *murder*. You can't ignore a thing like that, even when it's your auntie. You can't walk away from it. The game's on and you've no choice but to play to the end, even though it doesn't feel like a game any more.

Sunday morning I phoned Molly. From a box of course. She said, 'I keep thinking about that dream you told me. It worries me.'

'What dream?'

'You know – the one where you're walking in a lonely place and somebody—'

'Oh, *that*. That's nothing to worry about, Molly. I told you. That was just a dream.'

'Ah, well I'm not so sure, love. Your dreams . . .'

'Look. I don't walk in lonely places, right? Chance'd be a fine thing, with Dad insisting on picking me up wherever I go. No – what I'm phoning about is . . .' I told her there'd been no response to my latest notes. She said, 'What d'you *expect*, Kirsty? My anonymous phone call threw her off your scent. She'll be driving herself crazy trying to figure out who her persecutor is, now that you're in the clear. Why would *you* hear anything?'

I felt better when she said that. She's got her head screwed on, old Molly. When I asked her if she thought I should give Anne another poke she said, 'No, not yet. Leave it a while. Your auntie's pretty frightened, Kirsty, and frightened people have been known to confess, just so they don't have to go on being frightened. So leave it. Take a break. Concentrate on getting ready for Hallowe'en and when it comes, enjoy it.'

Good old Molly. I was glad I phoned her. Really glad.

# CHAPTER FORTY-NINE

Monday breakfast Mum said, '*What* incident in Mr Newell's class, dear?'

'Huh?'

'You know – you mentioned it in your letter of apology to Auntie Anne a week last Friday. Said you'd tell me later.'

'Oh, *that*.' Memory like a flipping elephant, my mum. I told her about the siren and my trance, if that's what it was, all those years ago. Dad was doing some last minute preparation so he wasn't there to hear. When I'd finished, Mum sighed.

'That's very strange, Kirsty. It certainly sounds as though you were given a glimpse into the past, but since that's not possible I'm inclined to agree with your auntie that the whole thing must have arisen in your imagination. Anyway' – she gazed at me – 'I think you ought to stop worrying about things that happened a long time ago, Kirsty, and concentrate on the present. And the future, of course. The past is the past but the future is *yours*.' She smiled. 'How's the costume coming along?'

'It's OK.'

'Good. The thing is, neither Dad nor I will be home Thursday teatime. Another of those interminable meetings, so I'm afraid you'll have to go to your auntie's for tea.'

'No!' I shook my head. 'No, Mum, I can't. Not Thursday. It'd mean carrying my outfit about all day in my bag, ruining it. Let me have a key, Mum, *please*. I'll get my own tea, change and go back to school at six thirty. I'll be OK, honestly. Let me, Mum. Just this once.'

Mum pulled a face. 'I don't know, Kirsty. Your dad—'

'You can persuade him, Mum. I *know* you can.'

'I'm not so sure. And he'd certainly insist on collecting you when this – rave's over. What time's it due to finish, by the way?'

'Half nine, and I don't mind being collected

if only I don't have to set off from my auntie's. Oh *please*, Mum.'

She sighed. 'All right, dear, I'll see what I can do.'

'Oh *thanks*, Mum. I mean it.'

I *did* mean it. Tea with Nefertiti, Thursday of all days? It'd have wrecked the whole thing for me.

# CHAPTER FIFTY

It's always a drag going to school. Goes with-out saying, but that Monday morning felt especially bad. I wasn't sure why at the time, but I know now. I'd only done a half-term at Fettler's, but half a term had been long enough to show me the difference between primary and upper school. Back at Cutler's Hill the coming weeks would be enlivened by a num-ber of events and activities leading right up to Christmas. Like, today they'd probably start making Hallowe'en masks and witch mobiles and covering the classroom walls with spooky pictures. They'd learn a Hallowe'en song and write witchy poems and stories. They'd have a *week* of Hallowe'en, not just an evening like us. And as soon as Hallowe'en's over, Bonfire

Night looms, so off they'd go making guys and bonfire scenes in collage and doing an assembly about taking care with fireworks. Then, before the ashes have cooled in the grey remains of bonfire heaps it's time to start learning carols and rehearsing the Christmas Concert and before you know it it's the holidays again.

Well, that's the way to do it if you ask me, but it doesn't happen at Fettler's. No chance. It's all revision here. Revision, tests and homework. Luckier than Sally Armitage up at Bessamer, but still.

Anyway, as I was wending my merry way through the allotments towards the all-weather pitch, breaking the school rule, Mum was talking to Auntie Anne on the phone. Unbeknown to me, she'd asked her sister to give me tea on Thursday before she'd mentioned the matter to me and now, having persuaded Dad to let me be home alone, she was cancelling the arrangement. Needless to say this was not breaking my auntie's heart, but it *was* telling her I'd be all by myself Thursday teatime, which happened to fit in perfectly with a plan she'd been hatching ever since she'd matched my two stamps. So in trying to do me a favour, Mum was actually setting me up for the worst encounter of my life. So thanks a bunch, Mum. I love you anyway, you know that.

# CHAPTER FIFTY-ONE

But anyway, things carried on in their usual boring way till Thursday morning when Miss Perrigo and her sixth form drama group started transforming the sports hall ready for the rave. Apparently they did something similar every year, but to us first year kids it was unbelievable. At break we stood gob-smacked as these seventeen- and eighteen-year-olds came staggering across the yard from the art block carrying the flats they'd knocked up out of four-by-twos and canvas. These flats were painted to look like sections of cave wall complete with fissures, slime and cobwebs. While one crew was erecting the flats all around the walls, another was busy on top of a mobile scaffold hanging spiders, bats and polystyrene stalactites from the roof. Miss Perrigo's area of expertise was lighting, and a mob under her was fixing great lamps onto gantries and running what looked like miles of cable down the walls and along the floor behind the flats. The buzzer went long before the job was done and we had to tear ourselves away, but you could tell it was going to be brilliant.

By lunchtime the hall was unrecognizable. We stood exclaiming round the main doors till this sixth-form prefect, Mossman, came and shifted us. 'You're in the way, you twisted pygmies!' she yelled. 'It'll all be here tonight, and you can gawp then till your nasty little eyes drop out. In the meantime get back behind the bike sheds, pick your noses and pretend it's just another day.' Terrific role model, old Mossman. I want to be just like her when I'm seventeen.

At hometime I came out of the cloakroom with Anna Buffham and Kylie Bickerdyke and there in the yard was a beat-up Transit in yellow and purple with MOBY DISK in white on the side.

'What the heck's that?' cried Anna.

'Sounds, you moron,' growled a passing year ten. 'For tonight.'

'You mean, there's a professional disc jockey?'

''Course. You're not in kid-school now, you know.' He jerked his head towards a knot of sixth-form girls round the sports-hall doors, which were closed. 'Simon flippin' Warner fan club, see?'

'How d'you mean?' asked Kylie, but the boy was striding away.

'Simon Warner,' said Anna. 'Our Steph talks about him. Reckons he's dead sexy.' Steph is Anna's big sister. She works at Marks and Spencer and goes to clubs all the time. 'Let's go over.'

A red-haired sixth-former with a fine crop of zits glowered at us. 'What do you kids want?'

'Same as you,' chirped Kylie. 'See Simon Warner.'

'Huh!' The redhead sneered. 'Simon's a man, not a teddy bear. He doesn't want little kids gawping at him.'

Kylie eyed the closed doors. 'Not exactly breaking the doors down to get to *you*, is he?' she growled. 'Pizza-face.'

157

You could tell this girl was sensitive about her complexion by the way she chased us halfway down the road. Kylie'd had to leave her bike behind. 'I don't care,' she gasped, when we'd finally shaken off our enraged pursuer. 'Don't need it tonight anyway. Not with my outfit.'

Anna looked at her. 'Coming by broomstick, are you?' We laughed, but I'd be laughing on the other side of my face in three hours' time. By golly I would.

# CHAPTER FIFTY-TWO

I had oven chips for tea. Mum seldom does chips, so it was sort of a treat. When I'd eaten I washed up to pass the time. Our kitchen window faces west. The sun was a fuzzy orange ball just above the trees. I could tell it was going to be a misty evening, just right for Hallowe'en. I left the dishes to drain and went upstairs.

I've got this eye make-up. Green, like the stuff my auntie uses. I washed, then did my whole face with it – cheeks, forehead, all round my nose and mouth. I did my lips blue and rubbed red lipstick on my eyelids with my little finger. Then I gave myself plenty of wrinkles with an eyebrow pencil and sprayed my tatty hair before standing back from the mirror to gauge the overall effect. It was wicked, though I say it myself.

Now for the costume. I'd taken an old black dress of Mum's, hacked it all round the hem and tacked on Grandma Kath's net so it sort of swirled round my shoulders and formed a close-fitting hood with a veil I could pull down over my face. Behind the veil my wrinkled, greenish complexion and red-rimmed eyes looked so dead real I couldn't stop looking at myself. I had on a pair of black woollen leggings and these high green boots with pointy toes and little buttons up the sides. I'd made myself a witch's hat out of black cartridge paper and bought a set of long black fingernails from a joke shop. With everything in place I switched out my bedroom light and damn near screamed when I saw my reflection in the mirror. That software was as good as mine.

The sun had set but it was only ten to six. I didn't dare sit down for fear of crushing Grandma's net so I went downstairs and wandered from room to room, watching the clock. Funny how time drags when you're wanting it to fly.

By five past six I'd had enough. 'What's wrong with arriving a bit early?' I whispered. I let myself out, hoping none of the neighbours would see me but since it was almost dark and the mist had thickened there was little chance of that. What I didn't know was that Auntie Anne had just set off in her car with the intention of catching me at home. So I set off, hoping to meet some little trick-or-treaters I could scare the pants off, but there was nobody about. I didn't fancy making a spectacle of myself along the main road, so I hung a left and headed for the allotments. It was strictly against the rules and Dad would've had a fit but witches don't give a toss about that stuff. It wasn't till I was in there among the unkempt privet hedges and narrow muddy paths that I recognized the landscape of my dream.

# CHAPTER FIFTY-THREE

You know which dream. Walking in a dark, lonely place. The one I told Molly was just a dream. Well here it all was, complete with hedges to snag my costume and the distant glow in the sky which was the floodlights on the all-weather pitch, switched on for the benefit of parents dropping their kids off in the fog.

As soon as it hit me I turned back. I did. You probably think I was being daft but *you* weren't there. You weren't *me*. Anyway, I started hurrying back the way I'd come, or trying to, but the net round my shoulders was catching on the privet. I had to keep stopping to free myself. You can bet I was scared. Really scared. It was all so like my dream that when Auntie Anne stepped out in front of me I wasn't even surprised.

I screamed though, I don't mind admitting it. Come face to face with a murderer in a lonely spot and you'd scream too. I tried to run, caught my foot in something, crashed through some privet and found myself backed up against a derelict greenhouse with Auntie Anne's hand clamped over my mouth. I struggled to tear myself away but she was leaning on me, pressing me into the crumbling brick. A crazy thought went through my mind. *Careful, you'll crush my outfit.* Here I was about to die, and some part of me was still after that software.

She was talking to me, hissing in my face. 'Listen. Stop fighting and listen to me, you stupid child.' I didn't stop. I knew I was fighting for my life. I grabbed her arm with both hands and tried to jerk it clear of my mouth so I could scream. The road was only yards away. People'd be passing. If I could just cry out someone was bound to hear, but she was strong. You wouldn't believe how strong she was. I tried to bite her hand but I couldn't find anything with my teeth, and then she punched me in the stomach. It was like being hit by a big bloke. The pain was unbelievable. I couldn't breathe. I wanted to double up but she was holding me and hissing in my face, something about a flipping doll. I was gasping and crying, plastering her hand with tears and snot. She was *killing* me, for Pete's sake. What had *dolls* to do with it?

Dolls. My dream. Two little girls. *The wrong way round*, she was saying. *You got it the wrong way round.* I knew then what she was on about, and she must have seen it in my eyes because she unclamped my mouth enough so I could choke out, 'What?'

'She sold *my* doll, Kirsty. Your mother sold *my* doll. She was like that.'

'Mum?' I gazed at her through my tears, shaking my head. The paper hat had slipped off and was on the ground. I felt it crackle under my boot. 'No she wasn't. Isn't. *You* are, and you're a murderer too. You pushed Grandma Elizabeth downstairs. I *know* you did.' My voice had risen. I screamed the words in her face till she clamped her hand over my mouth again. She was shaking her head.

'Wrong again, Kirsty, and it's no use scream-ing at me. You started this. You insisted on stirring up the past. You thought you knew the truth but you didn't, and now you *have* to know and you won't like it. You see, Kirsty, it was your *mother* who pushed your grandma down those stairs.'

'No!' I jerked my head from side to side against the pressure of her hand. 'You're lying. You must think I'm stupid. Mum could never do a thing like that. She's kind. Not like . . .'

'Not like me? Not like your wicked Auntie Anne?' she scoffed. 'Listen, Kirsty. Stop struggling and listen.' She removed her hand from my mouth. 'I'm not going to hurt you. Not physically. Any hurt you *do* feel you've brought on yourself by snooping.' She glanced about her. 'I wouldn't have chosen to do this here, Kirsty. I tried to catch you at home but you'd left, so this'll have to do. When I arrived at your grandma's house on June thirteenth 1983, your mother was already there and *my* mother was lying at the foot of the stairs. I'd caught her in the act, you see. My kind sister. She assumed poor Mother had altered her will as she'd said she would, but she hadn't. I knew that because I was in the habit of dropping in on her practically every day. Your mother hardly ever called, so she didn't know.'

'Why?' I gasped. I was bent forward, my arms wrapped round my stomach. I felt so sick and was trembling so badly I almost fell down. 'Why would Mum want to kill Grandma if the cottage was going to be hers anyway? It doesn't make sense.'

My aunt shook her head. 'No it doesn't, and it's no use asking me why she did it. Ask *her*.'

I shook my head. 'No. I don't believe you. *You* had a reason. You did it. You're just trying to get out of it.'

She sighed. 'If I did it – if it *was* me, Kirsty, why am I wasting my time talking? Why don't I strangle you and creep away before somebody shows up?' She shook her head. 'No, Kirsty. It wasn't me. I didn't deserve those notes. Those cruel notes. "Mummy's back".' She spat the words. 'Did you really imagine you could frighten me with superstitious nonsense like—'

It was then we both saw her, silhouetted against the glow. Grandma Elizabeth on her two sticks, hobbling towards us along the muddy path. 'Mummy's back,' she croaked.

# CHAPTER FIFTY-FOUR

With a hiss of indrawn breath my auntie took a step backwards, staring at the oncoming figure. A whimpering sound began which I realized was coming from me. As the hobbling woman drew near, the silhouette effect began to break down. Features became discernible. Black pits where eyes might be. The pale blade of a nose. A glint of teeth. I'd never seen my grandma of course, but this face seemed strangely familiar. Three more tottering steps and I had it. 'Molly!' I cried. 'How'd *you* get here?'

Instead of answering, Molly said, 'Get away from that child, Anne Tasker. If you've hurt her I'll . . .'

'Molly Barraclough.' Auntie Anne was trying to sound like she knew all the time but the silhouette had had her going, same as me. My heart was still thumping. 'Of course. I *thought* I recognized that voice on the phone.' She sneered at Molly. 'You fool, you've got it totally wrong, which shouldn't surprise me since you messed up practically everything you touched at Whiteleys. My sister Sylvia, remember? 'Course you do. Good, kind Sylvia. Well *she*'s the one you're after, the pair of you. *She* killed our mother. I'm just an accessory after the fact or whatever they call it, so you go right ahead. Tell the police.' She laughed briefly. 'You'll be doing me a favour, because to tell you the truth I'm sick and tired of guarding my sister's dirty secret.'

We went back to my place, the three of us, and waited for Mum to come home. I don't know how long it was because I was practically out of my mind. I remember running upstairs, tearing off my precious costume and rubbing and rubbing at the green on my face, believing that if I could just look myself again everything would be all right. After a bit Molly dragged herself up the stairs and made me put on jeans and a jumper and come down. She'd made tea. Or maybe that was Auntie Anne.

Anyway, Molly gave me a cup and I suppose I drank it, but I honestly don't remember, my head was so messed up. One part of me wanted my mum, another part hoped she'd never come. When I heard the car in the driveway I jumped up, ran upstairs and slammed my door. I heard Mum and Dad in the hallway. Dad laughed at something. These were the final seconds of their normal life and they didn't know. They didn't even *know*. I flung myself on the bed and wrapped the pillow round my ears so I wouldn't hear the voices which were about to wreck our lives. To make absolutely sure I wouldn't hear, I started singing very loudly a song they taught us at Cutler's Hill. A Hallowe'en song:

> *When stars appear and children sleep*
> *And witches round their cauldrons creep*
> *And Jack-o-Lanterns walk the night*
> *And bats and demons take to flight . . .*

Maybe you know it. Anyway, I lay curled on my side with the pillow round my head belting this out at the top of my voice, and I didn't stop when someone came in ages later and tried to pull the pillow away. I clung on to that pillow and kept on singing, even when two women I'd never seen before got me up and half-carried me downstairs and out to the ambulance. I remember the flashing blue light.

# Chapter Fifty-five

Mum gave herself up to the police. Well, three people knew her secret now and anyway she was sick of it. Sick of living with her conscience. I mean, just think what my nightmares must have done to her for a start. My little flashbacks.

I was four days in hospital, sedated. They sedated Dad too, at home, and they wouldn't let me anywhere near the court when Mum's case was heard.

Oh, it's OK. It was a few years ago. We're over it, I guess. As over as we'll ever be. She was in this open prison in Cheshire. Not a bad place, considering. We visited monthly, Dad and I. Sometimes Joe came too. He's a psychologist now and works at a prison, though not that one. He says people do bad things for all sorts of complicated reasons and we must try not to judge them.

I don't judge Mum. No way. I didn't know till Dad told me, but at the time she did what she did she was under a lot of pressure. They weren't living in the house I grew up in. They were poor, just out of college, living in a rotten, damp flat that had mice and was making Joe poorly. They were desperate to move but they couldn't afford anything right then. One day, listening to Joe cough and cough, Mum just snapped. She knew her mother's cottage was coming to her eventually but she needed it now. *Now*, for her baby's sake. She went out there with little Joe coughing and wheezing on her back. She didn't know Elizabeth hadn't changed her will yet, and anyway she didn't set out to kill the old lady. She hoped to persuade her to let them move in with her, but Elizabeth wouldn't hear of it. 'A *baby* in the house,' she had said, 'at my age? I couldn't bear it, dear. I'm sorry.'

And that's when Mum lost it and pushed her mother downstairs. She's not a killer. She flipped, that's all. She's always been a super mum to me and it was the happiest day of my life when she finally came home.

I never told her I'm *her* mum, by the way. I never told anybody except Molly. Me and Molly had a talk, and she said it might be wise to hang on to *that* particular secret. She's OK, old Molly, in spite of what Auntie Anne says. I know Mum wonders how I knew about Grandma Elizabeth and Grandad Bob and the Glory Hole and all that and so does Dad, but when they ask I mumble about dreams and visions. They probably think I'm crazy but I don't mind.

The dream's gone, by the way. My nightmare. I don't get it any more and you can bet I don't miss it. I like to think it's because Grandma Elizabeth's happy now but whatever the reason, it's restful. Yeah, that's the word. Restful.

Oh – you might be wondering why Molly showed up in the allotments that night in the nick of time, like Superman rescuing Lois Lane. I'd have wondered myself if I hadn't been so screwed up. I asked her a long time after, and she told me she'd worried and worried over the dream I mentioned – the one where I was walking in a lonely spot. She knew my dreams had a way of coming true and that evening, sitting at home imagining me setting off for the Hallowe'en Rave, she'd remembered the short cut through the allotments from when *she* was at school, and everything clicked into place. It was an amazing example of intuition, and it must've cost her a terrific effort to get herself across town in her condition, but I wouldn't half have been pleased to see her if my auntie *had* been bent on murder.

Anything else? Oh, yes. Kylie Bickerdyke won the software. Well – I never got there, did I? Anyway, her triumph was short-lived because Pizza-face and some of her cronies waylaid her in the toilets and chucked her in the pond. She floated too, apparently, which proves she actually *is* a witch.

Funny old world, isn't it?

## ABOUT THE AUTHOR

**Robert Swindells** left school at fifteen and worked as a copyholder on a local newspaper. At seventeen he joined the RAF for three years, two of which he served in Germany. He then worked as a clerk, an engineer and a printer before training and working as a teacher. He is now a full-time writer and lives on the Yorkshire moors.

He has written many books for young readers, including many for the Transworld children's lists, his first of which, *Room 13* won the 1990 Children's Book Award. *Abomination* won the 1999 Stockport Children's Book Award and was shortlisted for the Whitbread Prize, the Sheffield Children's Book Award, the Lancashire Children's Book Award *and* the 1999 Children's Book Award. His books for older readers include *Stone Cold*, which won the 1994 Carnegie Medal, as well as the award-winning *Brother in the Land*. As well as writing, Robert Swindells enjoys keeping fit, travelling and reading.

## BLITZED
### by Robert Swindells

*Imagine being alive before your
parents were even born!*

George is fascinated by World War Two - bombers,
Nazis, doodlebugs. Even evacuation and rationing has
got to be more exciting than living in dreary old
Witchfield! He is looking forward to his school trip
to Eden Camp, a World War Two museum. But he
doesn't realize quite how authentic this visit to
wartime Britain will be...

A thrilling drama from a master of suspense,
Robert Swindells.

ISBN: 978 0 552 55590 6